## "I GUESS EMMETT DOESN'T LIKE JEWS . . ."

She looked at me as if she thought I were joking and she was all set to laugh.

"No, I mean it," I said.

"I didn't even know you were Jewish, Bobby," she said. Somehow I felt it was the wrong thing to say.

"Why, does that make any difference?" I asked.

"No, of course not, don't be stupid," she said, but I was suspicious.

"You know, I've lived in Middleboro all my life, and I've always been Jewish, but somehow I felt that people judged me for *me* and not as part of a race or religion."

"They *do*, Bobby."

"No, they don't. Or at least, now I'm not sure. I'm not sure what you're thinking right now. 'Oh, God, he's Jewish, Daddy will kill me . . .' "

# *CHERNOWITZ!*

*"Involving . . . believable . . . an effective novel . . . exposes the mindlessness and insidiousness of prejudice."* —BOOKLIST

*"The power of this book is that it explores thoughts and emotions . . . unreasoned hate and prejudice and its effect on individuals today."* —JOURNAL OF READING

# Chernowitz!

by

# FRAN ARRICK

A SIGNET BOOK

I am grateful to Rober V. Lichtenfeld
for help and advice.
—F.A.

SIGNET
Published by New American Library, a division of
Penguin Group (USA) Inc., 375 Hudson Street,
New York, New York 10014, USA
Penguin Group (Canada), 90 Eglinton Avenue East, Suite 700, Toronto,
Ontario M4P 2Y3, Canada (a division of Pearson Penguin Canada Inc.)
Penguin Books Ltd., 80 Strand, London WC2R 0RL, England
Penguin Ireland, 25 St. Stephen's Green, Dublin 2,
Ireland (a division of Penguin Books Ltd.)
Penguin Group (Australia), 250 Camberwell Road, Camberwell, Victoria 3124,
Australia (a division of Pearson Australia Group Pty. Ltd.)
Penguin Books India Pvt. Ltd., 11 Community Centre, Panchsheel Park,
New Delhi - 110 017, India
Penguin Group (NZ), cnr Airborne and Rosedale Roads, Albany,
Auckland 1310, New Zealand (a division of Pearson New Zealand Ltd.)
Penguin Books (South Africa) (Pty.) Ltd., 24 Sturdee Avenue,
Rosebank, Johannesburg 2196, South Africa

Penguin Books Ltd., Registered Offices:
80 Strand, London WC2R 0RL, England

Published by Signet, an imprint of New American Library,
a division of Penguin Group (USA) Inc.

First Signet Printing, May 1983
30  29  28  27  26  25  24  23  22

Copyright © Fran Arrick, 1981, 1983
All rights reserved

Ⓢ  REGISTERED TRADEMARK—MARCA REGISTRADA

Printed in the United States of America

PUBLISHER'S NOTE
This is a work of fiction. Names, characters, places, and incidents either are the
product of the author's imagination or are used fictitiously, and any resemblance
to actual persons, living or dead, business establishments, events, or locales is en-
tirely coincidental.

    The publisher does not have any control over and does not assume any responsi-
bility for author or third-party Web sites or their content.

For Gwenn and Ed and Gordon

*This is the true story of Emmett Sundback and me . . . and how people are with each other.*

We live in a small town now, but when I was a baby we lived in New York, in the city. My parents had an apartment there when they first got married. And they told me a story about that apartment, about that building we lived in. They had a superintendent there who was very nice to them. He always fixed the plumbing right away and the doorbell and the air conditioning—stuff like that. And his wife used to love to babysit for me, too.

One time, my mother told me, they actually caught a burglar in our apartment when we weren't home, and my mother was so grateful, she and my father gave them a little reward. My mother also made a special dessert for them. That's when they said to her: "Mrs. Cherno, you're all right. You're quiet and polite and very generous, not like . . ."

"Not like what?" my mother asked.

"Well . . ." they smiled sheepishly ". . . you know."

My mother knew. They were saying, You're all right for a Jew.

They weren't evil people. But their minds had been set long ago. *How*, I wanted to know. *Why*, I asked my mother. People don't think lots of times, she said. They don't think rationally, historically, reasonably. They hear catch phrases and pass them on. Slogans. Hurtful names. And they do it more when they're afraid or helpless or deprived or insecure. There are times when fear is in the air more than at other times and then hate becomes catching, like the chicken pox.

My mother told me these things long before Emmett Sundback began to hate me. And even though I didn't think of them until after it was all over, I know they must have been in the back of my mind somewhere, about how mindless bigotry is . . . and hatred . . . and how much energy it takes.

Emmett had the energy to hate a lot. He needed to hate me. Or someone. I'm Jewish, but if I were black or gay or a member of any other minority, it would have been the same.

I know it's all thoughtless and mindless . . .

But it hurt so much. It hurt so much I wanted to do something about it.

# 1

I thought I was being so casual. But my mother still saw me leaving the house with the radio and tried to stop me from taking it—even though it's mine, and even though I bought it with the hardest-earned money I ever made.

"You're not taking that radio to school, are you, Bobby?" she asked, her voice rising.

I tried to divert her. "It's Bob, Mom," I said. "I'm fifteen, I can stop being 'Bobby' now."

But it didn't work, even though she smiled.

"I've been calling you Bobby too long to change now. Anyway, why are you taking that expensive radio to school? You're always telling me how things are stolen out of lockers all the time . . ."

"I want to show it off," I said truthfully. "I want everybody to see it."

"I just think there's no point in taking chances. Tempting anyone. I wish you wouldn't."

I kissed her cheek. "It'll be all right," I said. "Nothing will happen that I don't want to happen."

"Just be careful," she said and I nodded and left.

It's about a quarter of a mile from my house around the lake to the bus stop and for once I was glad about the walk and about the fact that it was cold out. Cold weather and walking are good for thinking. The sun was just beginning to come up and the snow crunched under my feet. All good omens: everything would work out.

I stuffed the radio inside my down jacket to protect the batteries. It felt hard and cold against my ribs but that was good, too. Everything was good, everything would work.

In my whole life, I never planned anything like I planned this. And all alone, too. I didn't consult one other person. But that's the way it had to be—it had to be all mine, otherwise I wouldn't be entitled to enjoy the results as fully.

I took a deep breath and shivered a little, but not from the cold.

When this works, I thought, it's going to be one of those all-time special feelings that only a few people ever get to know, and I'm going to love every minute of it because I really deserve it so much.

The face of Emmett Sundback floated into my mind—swam and weaved there, with all his features exaggerated and distorted, like in those carnival mirrors. His jeering eyes above his glob of a nose. They were ugly in real life anyway, but even more in this new picture I made of him inside my head. This time I didn't try to erase the picture like I usually do. This time I let it stay and I even enjoyed it.

My mother was cool this morning, I thought. She probably thought about Emmett Sundback, too, but she never mentioned him. She hardly ever asks me about him any more. She just waits until I bring the subject up if I feel like it. I respect her for that . . .

# 2

Emmett Sundback entered my life in junior high school. Our elementary school merges with three others when you get to junior high and Emmett bombed in from one of them, Oronco Pond. I didn't really know him the first two years, just saw him around. But last year in ninth grade we drew the same English class and that's when it all started up. I even remember exactly when: it was after a quiz, early in the year. He elbowed me on the way out of class and said, "Hey, Cherno, what'd you get on that?" meaning the quiz.

I said, "Why?" because there was kind of a funny tone to the question and also because we'd never talked to each other before at all.

"Because I asked you, that's why," he said. He was still using that same funny tone. It didn't sound threatening at all, but I felt threatened.

I answered him. I said, "Ninety." I'd really gotten a ninety-six.

"How come you're so smart, Cherno?" he said and he walked away.

He was smiling at me when he said it but it made me nervous anyway and that's the truth because I still remember it like it was yesterday. In fact, I don't think there's any part of it that I've forgotten . . .

"How much you weigh, Cherno?"

"Why?"

"Why are you always askin' me *why*, Cherno? I'll tell you *why*, Cherno, it's because I asked you, that's *why*, Cherno. Now do you know *why?*"

I looked at him with a kind of sneer on my face. At least I'd hoped it was a sneer. There are times when you wish you had enough chutzpah to say just the right thing, just the perfect thing, the thing that will reduce somebody instantly to a thwock of mashed potatoes, but you're really too scared, so you do it half-assed by sneering. Or trying to.

"I'm not sure what I weigh. About one-nineteen. Why—I mean—"

He laughed. "I guess you're not a wrestler, are you?" he said. "Too skinny."

"You a wrestler?" I asked, but he just grinned at me.

# 3

My best friend at the time was Brian Denny. He moved into the neighborhood when we were both in fifth grade. His house was on one side of the lake and I lived across from him, but we could see each other in our windows if we got up real close to the glass and we would send flag signals. We both liked the Beatles and we started guitar lessons from the same guy and we played on the same soccer team. He used to have to pass my house to get to the school bus every morning so I'd time my leaving with when I'd see him coming over the dam. After the second time I got needled by ol' E.S., I asked Brian about him.

"Hey, you know Emmett Sundback?"

Brian frowned at the dirt road. "Uh . . . Does he have black hair?"

"Yeah. Curly. It always looks greasy."

"On the big side?"

"That's the one."

"Yeah, I know him. He's in my science class. Why?"

"Because I *asked* you, that's *why*," I said in an exaggerated voice.

"Huh?" Brian said.

"That's what he says to me," I explained, "when I say 'why' to him. He asks me questions like 'How come you're so smart, Cherno?' 'What'd you get on the quiz?' 'What do you weigh?' Stuff like that."

"Why?"

" 'Because I *asked* you, that's *why*,' " I repeated.

"Oh." Brian nodded. "Well, he seems okay in science. I mean, he doesn't bother *me*."

"I wish he wouldn't bother *me*. You going to soccer practice this afternoon?"

"Yeah."

"Who's supposed to drive?"

"I dunno."

"I'll ask my mother if she can drive and then your mother can pick up."

"Yeah, okay . . ."

# 4

My parents are both in the "ed. biz." Education. My father's the principal of a high school down county and my mother's a French teacher. At least, that's what she was. Now she just substitutes, so she takes whatever class they call her for. She subs in my school, too, and I really don't like that at all, so since I started seventh grade we compromised about it: now she won't turn down a job just because it's Middleboro High, but she won't teach one of my classes. I guess it works out, even though she does have some of my friends in her classes sometimes. I'm *really* glad I don't go to the school where my father is principal. Anyway, at night when the three of us sit down at the dinner table and someone says, "How was school today?" any one of us could answer.

"Harriet's leaving," father said, sipping his wine.

"Harriet Strohm?" my mother asked. "But the school year's barely started. And she's been there for years. Why's she leaving?"

"Her husband's retiring. They're moving to Maine. How would you like a job?"

"Working for you? Uh-uh. I'd like to keep this marriage intact."

"Okay," Dad said with a smile. "But I figured you'd be mad if I didn't offer it to you first."

"Right," my mother agreed.

"How was your day, Bob?" Dad asked.

I didn't look at him. "Fine," I said. It had been, except Emmett Sundback stopped short in line going out of English, causing a pileup of kids with me first, smashing into his back.

Everybody had laughed, especially Emmett and including me. It wasn't a big deal, at least it was made to look like it wasn't, but I got this creepy feeling.

Anyway, I wasn't about to tell my parents my day was lousy because of that!

When I was in the fourth grade, some of the kids started picking on me. They were kids I'd grown up with since nursery school, even before for Pete's sake, and all of a sudden they were giving me the business. First they stopped talking to me. Then they'd get together in a bunch and point at me and start giggling and stuff. Once I even called one of them, Cliff Neimeier—we used to build blocks together—and point-blank asked him: "How come this treatment? What did I ever do to you?"

He was embarrassed, I guess. There he was, all alone on the phone with no other kids around to smirk with and he didn't know what to say.

Finally, he said, "You're spoiled. And you have to have things your own way in games."

After I hung up I thought it over. What did "spoiled" mean? I always thought it meant where you get everything you ask for from your parents. If that was the true definition, it sure didn't apply to me. I looked it up. Webster's fourth definition said: "To impair the disposition of, as by overindulgence." That's what I thought. I wasn't an "overindulged" kid. Had to have my own way in games . . .

I decided then to ask my mother. She'd known I'd been having some trouble but even back in fourth grade I tried to keep that kind of thing to myself. A matter of pride.

"Yes," she said immediately, "you do. I can see where it'd make the other kids crazy."

"I do not," I said. (Well, I was only ten!)

"Yes, you do. You come home crying that the teams weren't drawn fairly, or that they scored wrongly against you, or that they threw you out when you were safe, or something like that."

"But I'm telling the truth!" I wailed.

She shrugged. "Maybe. I can't argue that. But still, the other kids don't like that kind of behavior. You take games too seriously. They're only games, Bobby."

"But you should play them fairly," I insisted.

"Yeah," she said with a shrug, "but if they're fair enough for everybody but you . . ."

I thought about it. Maybe she was right. So what I did was to try not to complain any more, even when I thought something was really unfair.

And it seemed to work because everything was okay after that. I never had a whole lot of real close friends, but I had some, and besides, I liked to do a lot of things by myself anyway. And the next year when Brian moved in right across the lake, I played a lot with him. Things were going okay until Emmett Sundback started in on me in ninth grade.

# 5

"Hey, Cherno . . ."

He came up close to me and backed me against my locker. He was with another boy.

"Hi, Cherno," he said. I could feel my stomach churning. "Aren't you gonna say hello, Cherno?" He turned to the other boy. "He don't say hello, Eugene," he said.

Eugene said, "Yeah. How come you don't say hello?"

I gave them what I hoped was a disgusted look and turned around to open my locker. I didn't have any reason to open it again, I was finished with it, but it was there and it gave me something to turn my back on them for. But they still stayed there and talked about me to each other.

"Cherno," Eugene said. "What kind of a name is that?"

"Gee, I just don't know, Eugene," Emmett said. He almost sang it. "Hey, Cherno, what kind of a name is that?"

I made believe I was looking for something on my shelf.

"I said, what kind of a name is that, Cherno?" Emmett repeated.

I slammed my locker door and turned around, ready to move as I answered.

"It's a two-syllable name," I said and left while they were figuring out what two-syllable meant.

I walked quickly but not so quickly that they would get the idea I was running. Even though I was, in my head. My stomach was still eating away at itself and I felt like I was in some stupid TV show where the guy asks for police protection on a hunch the mob has a contract out on him.

Why me, I kept thinking. Why *me?*

School started to scare me. I thought about going to my advisor and asking to have my English class changed, but I decided against it. The school was big, but it wasn't that big, and I just couldn't give Sundback the satisfaction of watching me run. Besides, I didn't think it would stop him. That's when I began to sweat school.

# 6

About a week before Halloween, I was standing on line in the cafeteria and the kid right in back of me tapped me on the shoulder. It was a kid I barely knew but we had a study hall together.

"Hey, Cherno?" he said.

"Yeah?"

"Look, it's none of my business, but what did you ever do to Sundback?" he asked.

I took a breath. If it's possible to feel both exhausted and hyper at the same time, that's what I felt.

"I didn't do anything to him," I said. "Why?"

The kid—his name was Dave—said, "Because he's telling the world that you better watch out on Halloween. He's going to bomb your house."

I felt sick. "What?" was all I could say.

Dave shrugged. "I don't know. Him and his cousin Eugene were talking it around in homeroom. You know, loud, so everybody could hear." He shrugged again. "I just thought I'd ask you what you did to him."

"I didn't do anything to him. He's been on my

case since school started. I don't even know him," I said as I picked up my tray.

"He's a stupid slob," Dave said, as he paid for his lunch. "We were in Oronco Pond together and one time he tripped me on the playground. He stood there laughing like an idiot. I nearly broke my nose."

I started to walk with Dave to a table, but he saw some kids he knew and headed in another direction.

"Why'd he do it?" I asked quickly before he left. "Why'd he trip you?"

He began to answer me over his shoulder but seemed to change his mind in the middle of the sentence. "Ah, he's just mean," he ended up saying. "Watch out on Halloween." And then he was gone, sitting down at the table with his friends.

I sat down by myself at another table. I wasn't hungry any more.

Cliff Neimeier was the next one I heard it from. We were on the bus, going home.

He said, "Hey, Bobby, you going out on Halloween?"

I shook my head.

"Well, watch your house. Sundback's mouthing off how you're gonna be dead Halloween night."

"He doesn't even live in the neighborhood," I said, hoping I didn't sound whiny. "Why would he come all the way over here, anyway?"

"To get you," Cliff said simply. "That's what he says."

*     *     *

I heard it all week long. It really killed me that Halloween fell on a Friday because that meant all the kids would stay out later, without school the next day. I didn't know anything about Sundback's parents . . . Maybe they wouldn't care how late he stayed out.

Every night that week, we had the same conversation at dinner. It started out:

"Bobby, you haven't touched your chicken. It's your favorite! Are you sick?"

"Naw . .. "

"Well, then, eat some more, or you will be."

"Bobby, eat your pork chops, they're your favorite! Are you sure you're not sick?"

By Thursday night I had to laugh. Mom said, "Bobby, eat your spaghetti, it's your favorite!" and I couldn't help it.

"Mom, how can I have so many favorites?" I asked, grinning. "You've said the same thing every night, 'it's your favorite!' "

"Have I? Well, you normally eat everything so rapidly . . ."

"I told you, Rae," my father said, "it's a normal phase growing kids go through. One minute they eat everything in sight and the next—nothing." He waved his hand in the air. "Don't worry. Does he look undernourished to you?"

My mother made one of those twisted-lip faces but didn't say anything else.

I just couldn't eat. It was one thing to go to

school every day wondering what stupid remarks were going to be passed, and it was another to be building to something you *knew* was coming. Something specific. Like Halloween. I was scared, but I was pissed off, too. Emmett was forcing me to tell my parents. I would have to. They'd be home on Halloween and it was their house, too.

But I waited. I hoped it would blow over. On Friday morning, walking to the bus stop, I decided that if I didn't hear any more from or about Emmett Sundback and me and that night, I'd just forget about it.

But I did hear so I couldn't forget about it.

It was in English. Before English, actually. Just as I was sitting down at my desk.

"Hya, Cherno."

"Hya, Sundback," I said right back, looking him in the eye.

"You get the word about tonight?" He was smiling.

"What *word?*" I said sneeringly

He leaned over my desk and put his face right near mine, but I didn't turn away.

"You're gonna get it tonight, Cherno," he whispered. "If your house is still standing in the morning, you'll be lucky." He stood up then, grinned, and walked away toward his own desk.

# 7

"Who?" my mother kept asking.

"Sundback, Emmett Sundback," I repeated with a sigh. "Look, I really didn't want to mention it, it's so stupid. But I don't know what this kid is capable of doing—"

"But who is he?" my mother said again. "I mean, why is he picking on you? How long has it been going on? Did you do something to him? I never even heard the name before . . ."

"Sure you have," my father said. "His father's a local contractor. Haven't you seen the name on signs around here?"

"Oh. Maybe. I didn't connect . . ."

I was standing there listening to them and dying a little. I felt so humiliated, like I was back in fourth grade again, asking my parents for protection. I wasn't, I was only warning them . . .

"Well, what do you think we should do?" I asked, shuffling my feet back and forth.

"Maybe we should call the police," my mother said.

"Oh, man, *please*," I wailed.

"Now wait a minute," my father said. "I think we could call the local police and just ask them if they can have an extra patrol in the lake area because there was a rumor of trouble here. We don't have to mention names or anything, but it wouldn't hurt to know they're around."

I sighed. "Okay."

My father called. The police said they always have extra patrols in the lake area on Halloween, and what kind of trouble did my father mean.

My father said threats of damage to his house in particular.

"Yeah, kids . . ." the police officer said. "Everybody calls in with that kind of stuff."

"I think I should stay outside tonight," Dad said when he hung up. "It's a warm night, it won't be bad."

"I'll stay out with you," I said, feeling miserable and somehow to blame.

"Me, too," my mother added.

"Aw, not you, Mom," I protested.

"And why not?"

"I'll tell you why not," my father said calmly. "Because someone has to stay inside to answer the door when the little ones come trick-or-treating. You can't stand outside with a tray of candy apples like a sidewalk vendor."

That broke the tension a little and we laughed, picturing Mom hawking candy apples on the lawn in front of our house.

"Okay," she said, "but just be careful."

\* \* \*

By eight-thirty about forty kids had been by, and two patrol cars, driving slowly. Mom had run out of candy apples and was handing out those small-size candy bars and sugarless gum. Dad and I had seen no one except little kids and their parents, who stood at the edge of the yard looking bored to me even in the dark.

"Say, as long as we're out here, why don't we do something useful, like rake the leaves," my father suggested.

I felt relieved beyond belief. It might look dumb to be raking leaves practically in the middle of the night, but it was something to *do*. Something physical to do!

"Great," I said, and almost ran for the shed in the back where we kept our gardening stuff.

At nine we were still raking, with no sign of anything. But just as I was beginning to think it was all over—even the constant parade of little kids in costumes had begun to dwindle—I heard some deeper voices heading our way from down the road.

Dad heard them, too, and stopped raking for a second to look over at me.

I clutched my rake and listened harder.

There were a lot of them, I could tell by the noises. Every few minutes there would be a loud laugh and then low voices again. Guys' voices, not little-kid voices.

Dad walked to the edge of our yard, which was at the top of a slope. He was still holding his rake. I began to walk up toward him slowly, when the silhouettes appeared in front of us on the road. I quickly estimated about ten kids.

Anyone who knew him at all could've made out Emmett Sundback in that group, even though it was dark, because he was bigger than all of them. I was shaking, but at the same time, frozen. Everyone else seemed frozen, too: Dad, because he was waiting for the first move, I knew; Emmett and his gang because I guess they hadn't expected anyone outside there to greet them. It lasted for only a moment. Then there was some whispering and huddling among the gang. Next, they began to jeer and walk on. They all seemed to be yelling things at once so it was hard to make out any words, except for stuff I expected, like "Chicken!" and ". . . daddy to protect him . . ." and then they were gone, moving down the road past our house, making the same crowd noises we'd heard before.

My father turned toward me.

"Well, I guess that wasn't so bad," he started to say.

I shook my head. "It's early. They'll be back," I said, "when they think we've gone."

"Mmmmm . . ." Dad nodded. "Maybe. Still feel like raking?"

"I sure do," I said.

It was about ten-fifteen when they came back. This time, they weren't talking and laughing, but we could hear the sound all their feet made.

I could see that their arms were upraised, ready to hurl something, and that even though we might be outside it wasn't going to stop them this time. I heard a whirring sound as something whizzed past my ear and then cracking noises. I ducked instinctively, and when I glanced up, I saw the gang running down the road and my dad after them.

I looked around. It was eggs they threw; I thought it was. They were smashed on the walk and against the front door.

Mom was standing in the doorway.

"Eggs, huh?" she said, pushing open the storm door.

"Yeah," I answered. So far, I thought to myself.

"Are they gone?" She looked around. "Where's your father?"

Before I could answer, Dad was back, walking down the steps we put in at the top of the slope. He was panting. "I couldn't catch them," he said, shaking his head. "I just wanted to talk to them, especially that Sundback kid, but they scattered and I just couldn't get them. There was no sign of the police cars, either . . ."

"All right . . . come on in now, both of you," my mother said.

"I will. In a minute," I said. "I'm going to clean up the eggs before they dry."

"I'll do it, Bob," my father offered.

"No, you go on in, Dad. I'd really rather do it by myself."

My mother started to protest but my father nodded and both of them went inside.

I got a bucket from the shed, filled it with water from the outside tap and began to heave it against the places where the eggs had splattered. It took a while because I kept having to refill the bucket and some places needed more than one washing-down, but I didn't care. It was good to be doing something.

I was just finishing and getting ready to put the bucket away when I heard my name called softly from the bushes next to my house. I froze. There were no neighbors on that side, just woods—property owned by our lake association where members can dock their rowboats and Sunfish or pull them up on shore.

I wasn't about to answer. I kept on walking toward the shed. Don't run, I told myself. Don't run. The worst thing that can happen is they can drag you into the woods and beat the hell out of you, but even if they do, you can get in some licks and you won't show them you're a coward by yelling for your parents . . .

All this went through my mind in what was really a split second, because no one came out of the woods, not to grab me or for any other reason.

I saw something very bright fly through the air in front of me—far enough in front of me so that I knew it hadn't been aimed to hit me. I was staring at it as I heard the bushes being parted and fast footsteps crushing leaves as whoever it was raced through the woods.

The thing they had thrown was on fire. It was lying on the grass not far from the shed, burning itself out. I was close to the lake now, so I just ran over quickly and filled the bucket I was carrying with water, raced back and dumped it on the burning thing.

I could see it clearly now in the light shining from my living room window. It was about a foot long.

It was a cross.

# 8

I went over to our dock, sat down and stared at the water. It was a while before I could go back into the house and look at my parents.

"It's almost eleven-thirty," my mother said, looking up at the kitchen clock on the wall. "I'm sure it's all over now, aren't you, Jerry?"

My father said he was sure it was.

"Don't you think so, Bobby?"

I said I was sure it was.

I heard her saying, "This is the latest we've ever waited up on Halloween . . ." as I climbed the stairs.

I'd thrown the cross in the lake. Only one end of it had burned, the wood must have been too thick or too green for the entire thing to catch. They'd made it out of used sticks of lumber, probably left over from Emmett's father's contracting business. The sticks were held together with those wire ties you get in boxes of plastic bags. I stared at before I heaved it into the water so hard I thought I might hit Brian's house across the lake!

I knew what it meant. I'd seen the Ku Klux Klan on television, both in movies and on the news, wearing white sheets and hoods and burning big crosses and talking about white supremacy and Christian supremacy. I knew they hated Jews and blacks and Catholics and just about anybody that wasn't them.

So the cross on my lawn was because we're Jewish, and it made me more scared than ever because it wasn't just me any more that Emmett hated, it was bigger than me.

I don't know how to explain it. I only knew I couldn't tell my parents. I think what I felt was a combination of things: there was a kind of fear I'd never known before and it was also accompanied by an anger I'd never known before either. My parents, who loved me a lot, were upset because I was getting picked on. I knew they were worried. But if I told them—about the cross—they'd be worried in a different way, a much different way; part of me didn't want to lay that on them and another part of me was also afraid of their anger, especially my father's.

I began to think of all the things my father might do if he found out that what Emmett Sundback threw on our lawn was a lot more important than eggs.

Number one, he might call the police and/or the school principal, whom he knew. Doing that might be okay but then I'd still have to live with the repercussions. Number two, he might be so mad that he'd drive over there, to the Sundbacks', wherever they lived in the Oronco Pond school district, and if he got mad enough, he just might start punching out Emmett's father. Or Emmett. That, granted, was a remote possibility, but still, I'd seen my father get mad. Number three, he might start in on me again about defending myself, like he did back when I was in fourth grade. As much as he would have liked it, I just wasn't the type to take on one or more kids in a surprise attack, no matter how many boxing lessons he gave me. If they hurt me first there was no choice, but no one did and I never started it.

So while I sat there on the dock that night watching the moon light up the little waves on the lake, I made up my mind to tough this out myself. There was always help available, I felt secure about that, but for now this was between me and Emmett.

Monday morning I was late leaving my house for the bus stop but Brian was waiting for me anyway at the top of our hill.

"Hi," he said cheerfully.

I said, "Hi." I didn't feel like talking, and besides I hadn't heard from Brian all weekend.

"See your house is still here," he said, matter-of-factly. "Anything happen with Sundback on Halloween?"

"What did you do Halloween?" I said, changing the subject.

"Aw, I had to take Jordy around." Jordan Denny is Brian's younger brother. "My father wasn't home and my mother had to stay and give out candy."

"Oh."

"I saw them," Brian went on. "Sundback and his friends. Just as I was coming back home. They were at my house getting candy."

"They were trick-or-treating?" I asked.

"Yeah. Did they do anything to you? After last week, all that stuff he was yakking about . . . Ah, but he's just a big mouth, anyway."

Yeah, well thanks for all your moral support, Brian, I felt like saying, but I didn't. Okay, maybe he did have to take his little brother around so he hadn't offered to come over, but it would have been a nice thing to call up or something. I mean, he'd heard all the rumors, he knew what was going down . . .

I didn't say much to him, any more than I'd said to my parents when I finally went inside Friday night.

# 9

"I was at Middleboro today," my mother said one afternoon just before Thanksgiving.

"You were?" I said. "I didn't see you . . ."

"I got called in the afternoon for the health teacher. She went home sick."

I laughed.

"As a matter of fact, I did try to catch you before you got on the bus to give you a ride home, but you'd left."

"Oh, well, thanks . . ."

"I found out some things about Emmett Sundback," she said.

I didn't say anything. Ever since Halloween, my parents would ask me things like: Did anything happen with Emmett Sundback today? They didn't do it too often because I always said, "No, not really" even though he was making my school life a wreck.

"Don't you want to know what I learned?" my mother asked finally.

I shrugged.

"His parents are split. His mother lives over

in Oronco Pond and his father built himself a house, right here near the lake. Emmett lives with his mother, but spends time with his father here."

That explained why I'd seen him on the bus a few times. I thought he just rode it to torture me a little more.

"Where'd you get all this?" I asked.

"Oh, just nosing around. Don't worry, I didn't mention you."

I shrugged as if to say I don't care even though she knew I did. "What else?" I asked casually.

"He has an older sister who's studying to be a beautician. Nice girl, they say, keeps to herself . . . The mother's vague, she has a job somewhere, I don't know how much time she spends at home. Emmett's always been a troublemaker. A bully."

"Yeah."

"Does he pick on you as much?"

As much as when? I could hardly remember when he didn't.

"Well," I said, "he tries . . . I guess."

I guess. That day he'd come up to me before English. He had his cousin Eugene with him, which I knew was double trouble.

"Hey, Chernowitz, there's a quiz today," he said.

I knew there was.

"You all prepared, Chernowitz?" he asked. Eugene was grinning, next to him.

"Go haunt another house, Sundback," I said,

trying to sound bored. "You really make me tired."

"Make you more than that, Chernowitz," he said. "I didn't study for this test. Know why?" He looked at his cousin and smiled. "Because I knew if I sat next to you you'd push your paper over so I could copy it. Wasn't that smart of me, Chernowitz? Save myself all that time studying?"

I was already in my seat so I couldn't get up and walk away very easily. I opened my book and ignored him.

"See? I told you, Eugene. My old pal Chernowitz is going to get me an A," he said, full of confidence.

"Cherno," I said, looking up calmly. "Not Chernowitz. Cherno."

"Ohhh!" he said in an exaggerated voice. "It's Cherno, Eugene, not Chernowitz. Must be Italian, huh? Name ends in a vowel? That's Italian, right?"

The teacher walked in then and Eugene beat it, late, I guess, for whatever class he had. Sundback sat down at the desk next to mine.

Chernowitz! I ground my teeth together.

Our family name had been changed when my great grandparents came over from Russia. But it wasn't Chernowitz, it was Chanyakov. My father said that the officials at Ellis Island changed a lot of foreign-sounding names back then because they couldn't pronounce them. Sometimes they knew what the name meant in English, or sounded like it meant, and they just gave the people the English equivalent. We have cousins named Highland, not really a Jewish name, but a translation from whatever Highland means in Polish.

Anyway, my name went from Chanyakov to Chanya to Cherno somewhere along the line. It wasn't Chernowitz, ever.

The teacher passed out the test and I stared straight at it, never even glancing sideways.

First I heard him cough, little throat-clearings. Then they got louder. When I still didn't turn around, I heard his whisper: "Push your paper over, you kike, or I'll make you sorry."

I swallowed. Of course the words on the paper swam in front of my eyes, I couldn't see a thing. I'll fail this, I thought, I don't even know what I'm reading . . .

I got an idea. Sure, I'd fail. And I might as well take the reason for it down with me. I pushed my paper over to my right and began to fill in numbers at random for the multiple choice questions. Any old numbers.

"Atta boy, Chernowitz," I heard in a low whisper.

There was only one essay question and I don't even remember what I wrote for it, if anything. By the time it was over and the end of the period came, I was hating myself and feeling relieved at the same time. I never looked over at Sundback but I could feel a rush of air as he stood up.

"Good doggie," he whispered over my head. "Now you'll only get this." And as he walked quickly past my seat, he dropped a lighted match on my desk.

My reflexes are quick and I slammed a book on it right away, causing everyone to turn around and look at me like I was crazy. From the hall I heard a bark of laughter . . .

"Bobby?" my mother said, bringing me back.

"Huh?"

"You haven't been listening, honey. I said, what kinds of things does he do to you?"

"Who, Sundback?"

"Of course."

"Stupid things," I said. "Just stupid."

Emmett and I failed the quiz. The teacher was so shocked he called me up after class to ask me what happened. I was glad he kept me because I didn't want to catch Emmett's reaction in the hall afterwards, and I made up this big long story about how I was so sick that day, hoping I could drag it out until the bell rang and the next period would have started.

I did, too, only even though the hall was empty of kids, it wasn't empty of Emmett Sundback. He was still waiting there for me.

"The teacher didn't ask me why *I* failed, Chernowitz," he said. He was smiling. I didn't say anything. "You can afford it, a fifty on one quiz. I can't. I'm going to make you sorry you did that, Chernowitz, you smart little Jew-boy."

"Get the hell off my case, Sundback," I said, walking away quickly.

"Just remember," I heard him say behind my back.

That afternoon I saw him get on my bus after

school. Chewing my lip, I got on, too, deciding to get it over with. Three miles was too long to walk home, especially since it was freezing out. But nothing happened. He didn't even sneer at me.

# 10

We spent Christmas vacation in Florida, visiting my grandmother. My father's mother is the only one of my grandparents still living and we like to spend at least one vacation a year with her. Sometimes she comes to stay with us, but that's usually in the summer. She hates the cold weather.

At first I was afraid to leave, although I didn't say so to my parents. I thought for sure something would happen to the house if we went away.

I still had the fear on the plane, but when we got there, and the sun felt so good I started peeling off my coat and flannel shirt, the fear began to go away. In fact, I never felt better in my life.

My parents spent the vacation laughing and so did I. I think they were relieved to see me relaxed for a change, even though they never mentioned anything like that to me. Every time I took a second—and third and fourth—helping of my grandmother's cooking, my mother would beam at me and nudge my father.

We swam and we fished—I even went water skiing for the first time—and it was so warm and lazy and peaceful I just forgot about everything.

It wasn't until the plane was actually landing at Kennedy that I got that rush, that sickish, grabbing feeling in my stomach and I suddenly wanted to cry. It made me so ashamed. I wanted to beg my parents to turn back, get jobs in Florida, move right away, not even sell the house . . .

But I didn't. I knew this was a test. Nothing could last forever, anything could happen, things *would* happen . . .

I calmed myself down, literally, with deep breathing and careful logic. Emmett Sundback was a big fat bully, but he wasn't a killer or anything. So far, in all this time, with all his threats and remarks, he hadn't actually touched me physically. What he was doing was intimidating me and I was letting it happen. He was an insect, that's all he was, just an ant, trying to spoil my picnic of life. He was getting to me with psychological intimidation. Well, no more, not any more.

Just please, I prayed silently, let the house be okay.

It was.

The little girl across the street, who had a key and looked after our cat, Nasty, while we were gone, had been there every day and when my mother paid her she said everything was all right.

It was a good thing I was pretty rested from vacation because I sure didn't sleep that Sunday night, thinking about school on Monday.

# 11

"How was Florida?" Brian asked me as I joined him at the top of our hill.

"Great," I said. "How was it here?"

"Cold," he said with an offhand jerk of his head. He was walking quickly and I had to rush to keep up.

"Hey, what's your hurry?" I asked, but he just mumbled something about not wanting to miss the bus and kept moving.

When we got to the bus stop, Brian immediately joined Cliff Neimeier and a few other kids and I just kind of stayed by myself. I would have walked over to them, but I had a funny feeling that I wasn't so welcome. It wasn't anything they said or did, so I can't say why I had the feeling, but it was there. Once, Cliff looked over at me and then turned back to the guys. I told myself I was being paranoid for even noticing. When the bus came I got on with everybody else and sat in the back as usual, with the junior high kids, but it was a senior high kid who sat next to me and I was alone when the bus let the senior

high kids off. Was it my imagination or was
nobody talking to me?

"Hi, Neimeier," I said, bumping Cliff's arm as
we got off the bus.

"Oh, hi," he said and kept going.

Nah, I thought to myself. I'm really getting
crazy with this Sundback stuff.


English was fourth period. I spent third period worrying about it, which was stupid because Sundback didn't show. He was absent, or
cutting, or something. I had the best English
class I'd had all year.

Two periods later, at lunch, I got another
good break. Matty Greeley—she's a girl, Matty's
for Martha—came up to me on the food line and
smiled at me.

"Where were *you*, Bobby? You've got a gor-
geous tan!"

"Florida. Thanks," I said and smiled back. I
always liked Matty, kind of, ever since I first
met her in seventh grade. We had two classes
together then and two in eighth, but none in
ninth. Still I'd see her in the halls and always
watch her. She has this pretty hair that swings
when she moves and whenever I saw her she
always seemed to be smiling or laughing.

I didn't come right out and ask her to sit with
me that day, but I stayed behind her after we
paid for our lunches just to see if she had a
group waiting for her or anything.

She didn't. She looked around for an empty
seat, saw a bunch of them at the end of a table,

and headed for it, carrying her tray. After standing around for a minute to show I wasn't following her, I followed her and sat down in the opposite seat.

"Okay if I sit here or are you waiting for someone?" I asked without looking at her.

"No, fine, sit down," she said and began to poke into whatever it was the cafeteria was serving that day. I wasn't sure what it was and didn't care.

"Were you down there the whole vacation?" she asked casually.

"Yeah, my grandmother lives there. We usually visit her over Christmas . . ."

"Oh, nice. *My* grandmother lives in Middleboro. It's fun visiting her but—no tan."

I smiled at that, then had nothing else to say. I tried to concentrate on lunch and not on how her hair swung down the sides of her face as she bent over her tray.

"What's this stuff we're eating?" I asked finally.

She laughed. "I don't know. It's new. I don't remember anything yellow on the menu before."

"I guess it's not bad . . ."

"It's terrible," she said. "But I get so hungry by lunch time I'll eat anything."

"What elementary school did you go to?" I asked, apropos of nothing. I just wanted to keep talking to her.

"MacArthur," she said.

"Oh. I went to Middleboro."

"I know."

"You do?"

"Sure, I know where everybody went."

"How?"

She shrugged. "By their shoes," she said.

I wasn't sure if that was her sense of humor or if she meant it, so I decided that she was funny and laughed out loud.

She laughed too. "No, it's just that I used to go to Oronco Pond, so I know everybody there, then we moved and I went to MacArthur so I know everybody there, and now I know who's from Middleboro just by elimination. This is really awful, this yellow stuff, Bobby."

"Yeah, it is," I agreed. "Maybe it'll taste better when it turns green."

"Well, green I'll recognize," she said. "Green is Tuesdays and Fridays."

"You know . . . I'm sorry we don't have any classes together this year," I said, feeling absolutely bold by this time. After you laugh with someone you feel so much more relaxed!

"Mmmm, yeah," she said. "Maybe next semester."

"Maybe . . ." I was just about to ask if she'd like to go out sometime when she stood up and started gathering her stuff together.

"Bye, Bobby," she said with a smile and suddenly she was gone, heading over to the stack of used trays, with her hair swinging above her shoulders.

I watched her leave the cafeteria, hoping she might turn back and wave or something, but she didn't.

It could have been that she was just being

nice, being friendly, and would have been with any old Joe who sat down opposite her. But maybe she thought I was okay—after all, she was the one who spoke first, about my tan . . .

I wondered if I'd ever get up the nerve to ask her to go someplace, like one of the dances they were always holding in the gym on Friday nights.

But she always struck me as being one of those popular girls and so I probably wouldn't have a chance at all . . .

The thing is, with Sundback being out of English, and having lunch with Matty Greeley, it did turn out to be a terrific day.

I remember it because it was one of the few that whole ninth-grade year.

That night at dinner my mother asked if I'd had any trouble with "the Sundback boy" that day. I said no, that he'd been absent. I'd hardly mentioned Emmett Sundback at home since Halloween but my parents, especially my mother, still asked about him. I guess since I'm an only child, all their energies are concentrated on me so they pick up quick on whenever I'm sick or worried or unhappy or something that's even a little out of the ordinary. Or maybe it could be that they're just unusually perceptive, I don't know, but my mother guessed that Sundback was the reason I was having a hard time. She didn't know that I was also thinking about the other guys.

"Bob?" my father said.

"Huh?"

"I asked you a question, son."

"Sorry," I said. "What?"

"I was wondering how you felt about taking some lessons in the martial arts."

"Gee, I—" There it was again.

"Judo or karate or something like that. I don't think it would be such a bad idea, how about you?"

I shrugged.

"Come on, Jerry," my mother said as she re-filled my milk glass. "You're beginning to sound like those 'preparedness' people. You know, the ones who have fully equipped bomb shelters and arm their kids with automatic rifles!" She passed the bowl of mashed potatoes to me. I didn't want any but I started scooping.

"That's not what I mean at all, Rae," my father said. "I was only thinking of bolstering the boy's confidence, helping him gain a better self-image, know where he stands. Well, Bob?"

I mumbled, "I hadn't thought about it," and my mother took the empty potato bowl into the kitchen.

"Your mother hates anything she considers to be a violent act," my father whispered conspiratorially. I knew that. "But judo *isn't* really violent. It's graceful, actually. And I would like you to feel secure in your ability to take care of yourself."

"I know," I said.

He leaned back in his chair. "I used to box in college, did you know that, Bob?"

"Yes . . ."

"Your mother won't even let me mention it—"

He smiled and shook his head. "I did pretty well. Toyed with the idea of going professional. Of course, your grandparents were appalled, wouldn't hear of it . . ."

"Were you serious?"

"Oh, I don't know . . . But to this day I'm not sorry I know how to fight. I think you should know how, too."

That night I had fantasies of taking Emmett Sundback down, and making him so afraid of me his whole body turned to Jell-O whenever he saw me. But the fantasies wore themselves out. I wasn't sure that was the answer.

# 12

"You miss me, Chernowitz?"

Those were his first words, before English class started. This time he wasn't smiling when he said them. I saw a large black-and-blue mark on the top part of his forearm, sticking out of his tee shirt sleeve. I almost laughed out loud, thinking he got it from my own fantasies.

"I thought you died," I said, opening a book.

"Hah, you wish," he said back, but then sat down, in a different seat, away from me.

I thought, if that's all it's going to be, I can live with that. I can live with stupid remarks in English. Next year when they're making out the schedules, I'll make sure I have no classes with him . . .

Only that wasn't all.

# 13

Brian Denny started breezing right past my house in the mornings, instead of stopping and waiting for me if I were a few minutes late. When I saw him, I hurried to catch up and when I did, he was fine. Only . . . different.

"Hi."

"Oh, hi."

"How come you didn't wait?" I asked, coming right out with it. I know most kids hate that because it puts them on the spot and they get embarrassed. I hate it myself, but I can't help doing it. If you want answers to something, then how else are you supposed to get them except by asking directly?

Brian answered me, all right. "I don't know," he said. Great.

"Well, you always waited before this. What happened to change your attitude?" I said, pushing it.

"Nothing happened, jeez, Cherno—"

So then I talked to him about music and asked him if he were signing up for soccer again in the spring, and that he could deal with and seemed okay again. But when we got to the bus stop, he left me flat and walked over to the other guys.

It was around then that I found out I wasn't being paranoid in thinking that the kids I thought were my friends were ignoring me deliberately. It was really weird. If I passed one of them in the halls at school or on the street and I said hi, he'd say hi back. But if two or more guys were together, not only wouldn't they answer me, they'd sneer at me.

Brian started hanging around with Neimeier and some of the other neighborhood kids like Tim Kuhn and Chris Gustafson and Art Levoy. They were all in my grade and I've known all of them since we were babies, learning to swim at the lake's beach in the summer or learning to tie our shoes in nursery school. It's true that none of them were the greatest buddies the world could ever know, but I'm not the type of person who's "one of the boys" like that. I still played touch football and basketball with them when they'd get a game up in somebody's yard, or computer games after school, or soccer or something like that. And in the summer there was always someone to swim with or sail or fish. Now it was different.

Skating, for example. We live on a private lake and there are about two hundred families in our little lake association. There's always skating in the winter when the lake freezes, and we play hockey or have races.

Last January and most of February, there were kids on the ice all the time. Kids even rode bikes on it. I used to like to go out right after I'd come home from school to catch the rest of the afternoon light. Always before, there'd been guys to skate with.

Not now.

I'd skate over and everyone except the younger kids would skate away. If hockey teams were chosen, I'd just be left out, as if I were invisible or weren't even there.

And then it got more open.

At the bus stop in the morning, they started to talk about me out loud. They wanted me to hear. They'd mention my name and then there'd be a burst of laughter and some scornful or amused look in my direction.

I had never seen any of the guys in my neighborhood openly hanging around with Sundback, but the way they were being with me—the way they were treating me—seemed to coincide with his starting up the way he did. I really wasn't sure if there was a connection. Back in the fourth grade when I got this briefly, Sundback wasn't even around—he was tripping Dave Whatever, over at Oronco Pond, and didn't know me from Adam. So maybe this was just Pick On Cherno Year. A free-for-all, without anyone consulting anyone else, just going ahead on his own. Or maybe they got together over Christmas, while I was gone.

Sundback called me Chernowitz and kike and threw a burning cross at me. These neighborhood kids weren't saying anything like that, they were just being kid-mean, like in fourth grade.

It was strange with Brian. He was all with the other kids whenever they were around, but when they weren't and he was bored, he'd call me. I went every time he did, because I kept thinking that that particular call meant that the crap was all over or that even if it weren't, I had at least one friend in the world. But Brian would clam up every time I mentioned Sundback or even Neimeier. He'd just change the subject and talk about whatever game he'd called me over to play. I did finally get disgusted with him, but still I went when he called.

# 14

Any wondering I was doing about the connection between Sundback and the lake kids was finished toward the end of February when I saw them in the gym. There was Brian, Neimeier, Kuhn, Sundback and his cousin Eugene, standing together under the basketball hoop. They weren't playing anything, it looked like they were just using the gym to meet in.

I was there because I wanted to use the gym bathroom. It's the only one that isn't so filled with smoke you can't even see your own pee.

They seemed surprised when I walked in but they quickly turned it into something else.

"Hey, look it's him!" Sundback yelled with glee.

"Just the one we were talking about," Eugene shrieked, his voice bouncing off the gym walls.

Sundback left the group and walked toward me.

"We all decided you're a smart-ass kike, Chernowitz," he said while he was walking, but he said it quietly so no one outside our immediate area could hear.

"I don't give a damn what you've decided," I said, opening the bathroom door. Actually I wanted to smash his face in but I thought maybe showing him he was insignificant would be better. And maybe I was scared, too. All I wanted was to get into the bathroom.

"We don't like you, Chernowitz," he said, holding the bathroom door open after I went in. "We don't like you at all."

I went into a stall and closed the door, sat down and doubled over, pressing the heels of my palms into my eyes. Was it me or Jews he was after? Tim Kuhn was half Jewish, I knew that, so Kuhn couldn't be in on the Jewish thing. Could he?

It's not that my family was religious in the organized sense of the word. We didn't belong to a temple. We celebrated the main holidays, like Yom Kippur and Hanukkah but we celebrated *all* holidays—we gave Christmas presents, too. And when I was little, we used to have an Easter egg hunt with my cousins. There wasn't any religious significance to our holiday celebrations, they were just fun. I think my parents' attitude was that believing in God is okay, but when you start to make a religion out of it—

Well, it's like it's a personal thing. People should do whatever they want and let other people do whatever *they* want. I felt like a Jewish boy, but not any different from any other boy.

Now I felt different.

I hadn't heard the bathroom door close and for

all I knew Sundback was still standing there waiting for me to come out. What would he do when I did? Hit me? I began to think that wouldn't be as bad as what he was doing to me now.

I came out of the stall and the door was closed. But when I went out into the gym, the group in the corner was still there. Sundback said, "One, two, three" in a low voice and they all started chanting: "We-hate-Cherno. We-hate-Cherno," over and over, even after I was out of there and heading down the hall. I could hear them.

Stupid! Stupid, like kindergarten kids! Why did those other guys go along with it? Were they afraid of Sundback? Why would they want to suck up to him, anyway, it's not as if he were Mister Popularity, or the football star or anything . . . Why?

"Hi, Bobby!"

I looked up and blinked my eyes. Matty. Matty Greeley, coming out of the science lab.

"Oh—hi, Matty . . ." I looked over my shoulder to see if I could still hear the chants from the gym. The last thing I wanted was for Matty Greeley to hear them.

Matty was alone there, without her girlfriends, and I was alone—quickly, before I could worry about it, I moved closer to her and said in a rush, "Matty, do you think maybe you'd like to go to a movie sometime?"

It was the wrong way to do it. I hadn't seen her to talk to in over a month, and the first time we meet, all she says is hi and I'm asking her out. I felt like a fool. She looked at me like I was one.

Then she kind of chuckled to herself.

"Were you—was that—were you just asking me out?" she said with a smile.

I nodded. "Yeah," I said. "I guess it seems like out of the blue, but I've—really wanted to—for a long time."

"Okay," she said.

"Was that a 'yes'?"

"Yes!" she laughed. "Sure."

"Great," I said, meaning it. Boy, did I mean it. I started for the stairs.

"Bobby?"

"Yeah?" I asked, turning around.

"When?"

I licked my lips. You wimp, I said to myself, and came back to her.

"Friday?" I said. "I mean Friday, I just didn't say Friday, but I thought I said Friday. How about Friday?"

She shook her head, grinning. "Did you say Friday?" she asked.

"Several times, I hope."

"Okay. Want my dad to drive us? Or maybe my sister, if she's not busy."

"Well, I have to get a ride to your house, so my dad might as well just continue driving . . ."

"What's playing?"

I looked helplessly at her. "I don't know, Matty," I said.

"Well, it's okay, I haven't seen anything in weeks anyway."

"I'll call you, okay?"

"Uh-huh."

I bounded up the stairs three at a time. There is a God, I said to myself. And He kept Sundback in the gym, too!

# 15

Matty Greeley wasn't my first date.

In sixth grade they used to have square dances a few times a year and kids had dates for them. Also there was the fireman's carnival every year in June and we took girls to that, too. But this was really the first time I ever asked a girl to go out to something that wasn't organized, like the dances and the carnival. Because even though we went with girls, we were still in a big group. Now I was going to be alone.

I'm still not sure what made me ask Matty that day. Maybe I was feeling so rotten about myself that I needed confirmation of it, and Matty's "no" would have been it. Or maybe I needed a boost and I expected her to say "yes." I don't know, but it *was* a boost, all right, it definitely was. And nobody had to know about it, either.

My father drove us. The picture was a love comedy, I don't remember the title, but I remember we laughed at it. There's a Friendly's right next door to the theater and we went in afterwards. It didn't occur to me that I might run into anyone I knew, but it should have, since it was the closest hangout in the area. Sure enough, there they were—Sundback and Eugene—sitting at the counter when Matty and I walked in.

They didn't see us and there was a moment of indecision for me when I could have walked Matty right out. But if I'd done that, what kind of explanation could I have offered her? I held my breath and steered her into a booth, hoping they wouldn't notice us in the crowd. But it was a false hope.

"Hey, Eugene, look who's here?" I heard.

"Oh, look, there's Emmett Sundback," Matty said. "His father's finishing our basement." She waved at them. I leaned on my hand, rubbing my eyes with my fingers.

"Hi, Matty," Sundback said. He was standing over our table.

"Hi," she said. "Were you at the movie?"

"Nah, Eugene and me just hitched down. You out with him?" He was smiling.

"No, we just happened to sit down in the same booth," I said lamely, trying to prevent Matty from answering him.

"You got better things to do than hang out with this creep-o, Greeley," Sundback said, with his cousin leering behind him.

Matty stopped smiling then, and picked up a menu.

"Crawl back in your hole, Sundback," I said. "You're not wanted here."

His arm flew out, knocking over a glass of water that had been left on the table by a previous customer. I moved away quickly as it started to dribble over the side onto my lap. Matty leaped up and began to catch the water in a napkin and I vaguely heard Sundback saying, "Aw, hey, I'm sorry about that, tsk tsk, boy, am I clumsy" as both of us ignored him in our cleaning-up efforts.

"I'm sure the waitress will bring you more water, Chernowitz," he said before he was forced out of the aisle by a family putting up a high chair at the next booth.

"Why did he do that?" Matty asked.

"I'm not sure," I said.

"What did he call you? Chernowitz?"

"Yeah, I guess so."

"Why'd he call you that? Is that your real name or something?"

"No. My real name is Cherno . . ." I looked straight at her. "I guess he doesn't like Jews," I said.

She looked back at me with her head tilted and her mouth partly open as if she thought I were joking and she was all set to laugh.

"No, I mean it," I said.

"I didn't even know you were Jewish," she said. Somehow I felt it was the wrong thing to say.

"Why, does that make any difference?" I asked.

"No, of course not, don't be stupid," she said, but I was suspicious.

"You know, I've lived in Middleboro all my life," I said, "and I've always been Jewish, but somehow I felt that people judged me for *me* and not as part of a race or religion."

"They *do*, Bobby."

"Want to order now?" the waitress said, standing there crisp and cute in her blue checked apron.

"No, they don't," I went on. "Or at least, now I'm not sure. I'm not sure what you're thinking right now. 'Oh, God, he's Jewish, Daddy will kill me . . .' "

"I am not, cut it out, Bobby."

"Hey, you want to order now?" the waitress persisted, licking the tip of her pencil.

"Maybe it is my fault, I don't know," I muttered. "What do you want? To eat, I mean?"

Matty glanced up at the waitress and back at me again.

"Look, you have to order because we're getting backed up here—"

"Okay, a hamburger and a small Coke," I said, wondering how I'd ever get it down. "What would you like, Matty?"

"I don't know," she said, "I guess I'm not hungry. Just a Coke."

"Do you know him very well?" I asked. "Sundback?"

"No . . . Sometimes he helps his father work. So on weekends I've seen him at my house. They just finished building us a garage and now they're doing the basement. I didn't know him well when I was at Oronco Pond, either. I really wouldn't let him get to you, Bobby."

I mumbled, "Yeah," but the evening was spoiled for me even before what happened next. When we got through eating, I went to call my father to pick us up but I had to fight off Sundback who was sticking his finger in the dial or pushing down the receiver holder, so I couldn't get through. He kept laughing and ducking and I kept trying to call and keep him out of my way at the same time and finally, Matty had to call and I was so damned humiliated I thought I'd never get over it. I still cringe, even now, even though it was a year ago almost.

# 16

I was about as low as I could get and didn't think things could get much worse, but lots of times when you think things can't get worse that's when they do and they did.

My grandfather, may he rest in peace, always used to tell me: "Ninety-nine percent of the things you worry about never, never happen." I guess that's true, only it's the things you *don't* worry about that sock you in the face.

Emmett Sundback moved in with his father. Right here, on the lake. I guess it was toward the end of March, beginning of April. Which meant that not only was I going to get a doseful of E.S. at school, I'd also get the privilege of two bus rides and a possible chunk of him on my home turf.

The bus ride in the morning was the most fun. Everybody'd be standing there at the edge of the dirt road where the bus picked up the lake kids and then the ninth-grade boys would get in this huddle and make jeering remarks about me. Then one of them would come over and grab at my hat and they'd toss that around for a while until it landed in a tree. I was glad it was nearly the end of cold weather, so that'd be one less thing they could grab. They also got my books, which made me learn to fold my homework and keep it in my inside pockets instead of in the pages of my books. If I had an art project or something like that, I'd ask one of my parents to drive me to school because if they didn't, the project would get wrecked for sure.

The thing I hid from my parents was how bad it was—in other words, the degree of torment. Terrorism? That's probably going too far, but there's a legal term I've heard of called "mental anguish" and I really had a good share of that.

I think that in spite of all Sundback's crap, the thing that hurt me the worst was Brian Denny, my "best friend," who said, as we were getting off the bus at school one morning: "Move over, Jew bastard, you take up too much room."

It shocked me so much I couldn't breathe for a minute.

Sundback was standing with him and they both burst out laughing when Brian said what he said.

And next: Every time I'd pass one of the guys in the halls or anywhere in the school, I'd get bumped, or pushed, and whoever did it would make a sound, "ccchhhhhhhh," like the beginning of a sneeze. At least, that's what it sounded like to me until I realized that what they were saying was "Jew" in a snide, whispery way. I found that out when Emmett was the one who pushed me because he really said "Jew." The other kids, Kuhn, Neimeier, Gustafson, Levoy and even Brian—they never said it outright. They never said "Jew." Brian had said "Jew bastard" that one time when Sundback was around to hear him but he didn't say it when he was alone. And Kuhn, for Pete's sake—I really wanted to tell his father. Or mother, whichever one was Jewish. That was really scary that he should be in on it, too. Didn't he know what it meant?

Everything was so simple to me before. You're supposed to judge all people individually, right? If you're a crummy person, people won't like you, whatever color or religion you are. If Sundback thought I was a crummy person, okay, but if he hated me just because I happened to be Jewish, then I didn't know what to do about it. And if Sundback was able to get everybody to go along with him just because he was a bully, then how could I ever get it sorted out logically?

I don't know, I still don't know. All I know is that I was so frustrated, not being able to do anything about what was happening, that the only thing I felt I could do was try to make sense out of it and I couldn't even do that.

I was still embarrassed to look at Matty Greeley, so now instead of looking for her I just tried to avoid her. I was trying to avoid everybody. Home was the only place I felt safe and even that wasn't completely secure because I had to put on an act for my parents. Things were humiliating enough without going through it with them, and besides, I just didn't know what they would do about it and knowing my father, something would be done about it. Only from him, not from me, and I just couldn't stand that.

# 17

There was a note being passed to me in English. The teacher had stepped out for a minute and in the usual noise that accompanies something like that, I looked up and saw this piece of folded paper being passed toward me from the back of the room, from Sundback.

I sighed, waiting for it to get to me, wondering what I'd do with it when it got there—would I read it or just crumple it up? In those few seconds I decided to crumple it up and throw it at Sundback, but also in those seconds, the teacher came back in and focused right on Marty Ewell passing the note to Sandy Pintak who was supposed to pass it to me.

"I'll take that," the teacher said and without breaking his stride walked over to Marty and took the note. He opened it up, looked at it, and frowned. He scowled down at Marty.

"This your work, Ewell?" he asked.

Marty, who didn't know what was even in the note, looked panicked.

"No, *sir*," he said. "I was just passing it."

"To whom?"

The whole class was quiet.

"Uh," Marty shrugged his shoulders. "Just around," he said. "Someone just handed it to me, I was just passing it on. I don't know what it says, Mr. Shafer."

The teacher looked around the class but only a few kids looked back at him.

"Will anyone tell me from whom this . . . this note originated?"

Of course not, you jerk, I thought, rubbing my eyes.

"For whom was it intended?" Mr. Shafer asked.

No one spoke. Did he really expect them to?

Mr. Shafer crumpled the note, but he did it by smacking his two hands together with a loud crack. Then the room was dead silent while he glared at everybody in it. I looked around, too, out of the corner of my eye, and I saw Sundback looking innocently up at the teacher. No one was going to point a finger at him. And now, no one but Sundback and the teacher would know what was in the note.

There was an old story I heard once when I was a kid in camp and they used to tell ghost stories around a campfire. This one was about a man who was given a white card by some unknown woman on a busy city street. The card was written in a foreign language that the man couldn't understand, but whenever he tried to get it translated, something awful would happen to him and he never could find out what was written on the card. Finally, after he lost his job, his wife, his kids and his house, he met the woman again on the street—the one who had slipped him the card in the first place. He ran after her, followed her home, begged her to see him and tell him what was on the card. Finally, after days and days of hanging around, begging and pleading, the woman consented to see him. Only just as she was about to tell him what was on the card, she had a coughing fit and died. And with her last breath, the words faded from the card.

I thought about that story as I watched the teacher, Mr. Shafer, turn quickly around, march to the front of the room, face the class again and while still scowling, rip the note into tiny pieces and drop them into the big green wastebasket near his desk. I sighed. The writing faded from the card.

"You will spend the remainder of this period taking an impromptu test. I hadn't planned this, so I'm going to give you one question from your final exam, which you may omit then if your answer is satisfactory now. Take out your copies of *The Merchant of Venice.*"

Everybody groaned, but when Mr. Shafer looked up and glowered again, they stopped. I really wondered what was in Sundback's note.

# 18

Sundback was pretty cool for a while after that, at least in English. I guess he was scared of Mr. Shafer, and he was doing so badly in the course he couldn't take any chances.

But he was harder on me outside of school, and he had more opportunity, now that we were on the same school bus.

Brian Denny left for school a good ten minutes earlier than usual every day; I could see him coming over the dam at seven o'clock instead of ten or a quarter after. I knew he was doing it to avoid me, but that was fine with me. I also had the satisfaction of knowing he had to get up earlier to do it, because if he hadn't, then I would have. I was timing my own walk to get to the bus stop just as the school bus was pulling up. Once I missed it and had to get driven, which was also okay with me, though I sure wouldn't have done that on purpose and let everyone think my mom had to take me to school.

Brian stopped calling me also and when soccer began again in mid-April, our mothers had to drive us separately. Mine asked me about it but I just said Brian was a nerd and I didn't want to mess with him any more, and I was sorry about the car pool loss.

"You know, Bobby," she said, "you seem to be having a problem with your social life."

"What do you mean?"

"Well, there's that business with the Sundback boy—is he still bothering you?"

"Yeah, a little . . ."

"And now you've had this falling-out with Brian—you used to be close—and I haven't seen you bring anyone home in so long, or go anywhere—whatever happened to Tim or Cliff or—"

"Ah, they're all nerds," I said.

She pursed her lips. "It isn't good, Bobby. . ."

"Bob," I said.

"Bob or Bobby, one or both of you has a problem! Don't think we haven't noticed a change in you this past year, either."

"I'm okay," I mumbled.

"Look," she said, touching my arm, "I know what it's like not to want to tell your parents every little ache and pain. But something's wrong when a boy your age—smart, nice-looking, good sense of humor—"

I smiled and made that gesture comedians make when they want more applause.

"No, really, Bobby, I wonder why you don't seem to have a single friend. It can't be that everyone is a 'nerd.' Some of it has to be you."

"I like to be by myself," I said feebly.

"Well, fine, so do I, but not every minute of the day."

"I'd like it every minute of the day," I grumbled.

"No, Bobby—"

"Look," I said, "I'm playing soccer, it's a team activity. Brian Denny isn't the only kid on the team, so I'll be with other kids. There's practice twice a week and games on Sunday, okay?"

She said okay. What else could she say? I just couldn't tell her any more. It was my problem and I wanted it to stay that way if it had to stay at all.

Emmett Sundback didn't play soccer. I was sure it was because he was too slow and I would've bet there wasn't any one around to drive him to practice and games. He was a wrestler, that's what he liked, and all I hoped was that I never had a gym class with him.

I was glad about soccer when it started. Brian and Tim Kuhn were the only lake kids on our team, but that was because in ninth grade you had a choice of either playing A.Y.S.O. or ninth-grade soccer and a lot of them played through the school. I stayed with A.Y.S.O. and most of my team were eighth graders.

It was all physical, we were all over the field, so I hardly came in contact with Brian. He never rejected a pass because it was me kicking it, naturally, and he never deliberately wasn't there to back me up if I needed it, either. So I guessed that the rules for Hating Cherno were suspended during a sport.

One time I almost laughed. I kicked a goal. It really was an accident, the ball bounced off the heel of my cleat and line-drived itself right into the net, surprising the goalie and especially surprising me. The parents on the sidelines began to cheer—I could hear my father's bellow—and, of course, my teammates did, too. And I saw Brian come up with a big grin ready to clap me on the back, suddenly change his mind, mid-grin, and walk away, clapping another kid on the back with the hand he'd already raised for me.

"You ass, Denny," I said to myself. "You stupid horse's ass!"

My father had been watching the game with Brian's dad and when it was over and we had won by one goal, they both came over to me.

"Hey, that was terrific, Bob," Mr. Denny said.

I didn't say it was an accident, though I had been about to. I said thanks.

"Hey, Brian, wasn't that great?" Mr. Denny said. Brian was eating an orange and nodded, not looking at either of us. "Come on, you guys, whatever's been bugging you, why don't you shake hands and forget it right now?"

I bit my lip and looked at the ground. I guessed Mrs. Denny wasn't crazy about the car pool loss, either.

"Well?" my father said, standing next to Mr. Denny.

Brian spit out a seed. "Nothing's bugging me," he mumbled.

"Me neither," I added.

"Well, then . . ." Mr. Denny said. "Well, then. Good. Glad to hear it."

But your wife will still have to drive Brian to practice, I thought.

# 19

It was bad, waking up every morning with a soggy cloud hanging over your day. Spring had come, which always made me feel so good before. Now I hated it, because nobody was so intent on hurrying into buses and buildings any more, or huddling inside his own jacket or his own space. Now the kids moved around, stayed out longer, felt freer and acted that way. Before, when I'd get to the bus stop just in time to walk on the bus, the kids would be clustered together, shivering, and looking up and down the road for the bus's arrival. When the warm weather came, they spread out. Some of them were way up my road, ready to meet me coming down. They didn't touch me, but they'd fall in right behind me, and I mean *right* behind, dogging my footsteps, kicking my shoes with theirs while they walked and snickering when Emmett and Brian would say things like "C.K.C.—C.K.C." in a chant. It meant "Christ-killer Cherno," which Sundback let me know up front, so they could chant it out loud without anyone else understanding it. Then they'd chant it on the bus, like a school cheer, so that even the seventh and eighth graders picked it up, giggling, not knowing what it meant, but feeling big-shot. After a while the bus driver would shut them up, but they'd made their point and I'd hear "C.K.C." all over school.

I still managed to keep my grades up in everything except English, my best subject, but that was because I was afraid to open my mouth any more and my class-participation grade dropped like a stone. Mr. Shafer spoke to me about it a few times and each time I just said I'd try to do better but I didn't and he quit talking to me when all I did was clam up. I felt bad because I knew he was really trying, but I still wasn't about to say anything to him.

It got even worse when my mother told me that Mrs. Denny had called Mrs. Kuhn about a car pool to soccer and then Mrs. Kuhn called Mom and they worked it out that the three of them would drive back and forth.

"So now I have to ride with Brian and Tim both?" I asked, feeling like my stomach was a lead ball. "I didn't even know Mrs. Denny knew Mrs. Kuhn." The Kuhns live two back roads up from the lake.

"Well, she didn't, but she found out that there was another kid on your team from the lake area and decided it was silly not to take advantage of it. Milly Kuhn called me because *she* thought it was silly, too. After all, there are three of us and with everyone's time limited, not to mention gas prices—"

I turned away. I had to lean on the table. I felt dizzy.

"Oh, come on now, Bobby, it's only a ride, back and forth from the Oronco Pond field twice a week. Now maybe you don't like these boys any more, but can't you live with that to save me a little extra time and money?"

They hate Jews, Ma, can you live with *that?* But I only said it in my head.

I could quit soccer, I figured. But I really didn't want to and besides, how could I explain it.

All right, what could happen with somebody's mother right in the front seat all the time?

"Okay," I said, finally. "Okay, okay."

"Bobby, you know, you could make an effort to get along with these boys. You were once such good friends, why, you and Timmy Kuhn were in nursery school together, you've been all through grade school together. Whatever happened to change your attitude like that?"

I shook my head helplessly. That was when I came closest to telling her, but I knew it was *my* problem and *my* responsibility. My parents deal with the community all the time. How would they feel, knowing . . . knowing . . .

Absolutely not. I wouldn't say anything unless something happened that affected them. And nothing had and I felt sure nothing would, either. I'd gotten the feeling that Sundback wanted no problems with adults; nothing he'd ever done to me was in the presence of an adult. And I remembered Halloween, which I was sure would have been much worse if my father hadn't been outside the whole time.

The rides to practice were bad but bearable. Brian and Tim would sit bunched together and talk only to each other, usually in whispers. When my mother drove, I'd sit in front and stare straight ahead. It just killed me when my mother would be so friendly to them.

She'd say, "Well, how's school, Brian? Your mother tells me you're a real math whiz!" Or, "We haven't seen you at the house in so long, Tim, why don't you stop over sometime soon?"

Then one would nudge the other and grin or wink and say, "Oh, yeah, Mrs. Cherno, school's fine" and "Yeah, I'll come over real soon!" And then I'd have to hear it later about why didn't I make an effort to join the conversation?

The one good thing about the spring was the opening of the baseball season. I'm a New York Mets fan and have been ever since I was a little kid and the Mets won the pennant. They haven't done too much since, but I guess they made such a big impression on me back then—my father was yelling and cheering so much—that I've been a fan since. Maybe the only one left . . .

So the crummy days were relieved by the nights—about two or three a week—when I could watch a Mets game on television. During the winter I had kept up with all the wheeling and dealing from the newspapers and sportscasts and I knew everything about all the players, from their batting averages to their shoe sizes, practically. It was good to watch them in action again, even though they lost their first four games.

The Mets were also an excuse for me not to be out playing ball or fishing with the guys like I used to do. I just said I'd rather watch the Mets game, and for sure, none of the other kids wanted to do that!

My parents continued to mess me up without knowing it. One morning my father was lugging the trash cans up our hill for collection—usually I did it—and he met Mr. Denny out for his morning jog.

"I didn't know you jogged, Charlie," says my father . . . "Only in the nice weather, Jerry, ha ha," says Mr. Denny. "Good for getting all that winter fat off, eh?" says my father. "You bet, how about joining me?" says Mr. Denny and so my father started jogging around the lake every morning with Brian Denny's father.

"We thought it would be nice if you and Brian joined us," my dad said after he'd been at it about a week.

"Brian jogs at night," I said. "I've seen him."

"Well, he's going to jog in the morning now. With his father. And us."

"This isn't a good idea, Dad," I said. "Brian and I really don't get along any more. Just let it be."

My father came and stood over me. "Now look, Bob. All this is, is a father-and-son activity. Some healthy exercise. You can use it, I can use it. A couple of soccer practices a week aren't enough to get you into good shape. Now how about it." There was no question mark at the end of that sentence, so that was that.

I guess that Brian couldn't get out of it either because the next morning, before work and school, the Dennys showed up at the top of our hill in sweatsuits. The two men took off instantly, leaving Brian and me standing there stupidly kicking dirt.

I followed after a second and so did Brian and the four of us did make it around the lake, except it ended up with my father and me pretty far behind the Dennys. I guess we were more out of shape than they were. Finally, my father called, "Say, that was great, Charlie!" and barely staggered into the house. I had to help him into the shower, with my mother sitting up in bed, laughing hysterically.

Naturally, Brian used the experience against me so he could play Big Man with the other kids. Slapping his thighs and carrying on, he talked loudly about how really weak we are, my father and I, and how he and his father were practically around the lake three times to our once.

Sundback, all ears, turned all mouth later.

"You Jews are all weak," he hissed at me outside English. "You use all your energy conning teachers and counting your money, right, Chernowitz?"

I swallowed. "Well, somehow we found time

to kill Christ, right, Sundback?" I said through clenched teeth.

His face turned red and his eyes got narrow. He raised his hand as if to hit me and I was almost welcoming it, when he just turned and stomped into the class.

I was sorry I said what I said. I knew it wasn't true about the Jews having killed Jesus, but a lot of people still believed it or wanted to and, anyway, *I* wasn't the one who did it.

I stayed out in the hall after the bell rang, leaning up against the wall, trying to think.

I had always been brought up to respect other people, whatever they were. No matter how mad I got at anyone, it never would have occurred to me to call them by an ethnic name. But if other kids did, then maybe they weren't brought up the same way I was. Maybe they got prejudice from their parents. Maybe Sundback's parents hated Jews. Maybe Brian Denny's parents did, too, only they knew better than to show it.

Maybe I didn't trust anybody at all any more.

# 20

Brian went back to jogging in the evenings. He didn't show up mornings with his father any more and I wondered if that caused some kind of big fight between them.

But Mr. Denny said, "Brian prefers his evening jog. He says it's cooler then."

I had to laugh at that because even Mr. Denny was running in place to keep warm that morning.

"Well, you know how sticky it's been most times," he said sheepishly.

"I sure do know how sticky it's been," I said and looked right at him.

He didn't duck it. "Your father and I were hoping you boys could patch up whatever's been between you," he said.

I couldn't help it. I said, "You know what's 'been between us,' Mr. Denny?"

Man, I wanted to bite off my tongue. There we were, in front of our house: my father looking at me hard; Mr. Denny looking at me quizzically. I was sorry I said that, what was I going to say now . . .

I gripped the rusted iron railing at the top of the steps. In my head, the words sounded fine. Your son, Mr. Denny, has no mind of his own. He has no sense of loyalty or friendship and besides that he's a stinking anti-Semite, did he get that from you?

"What?" I said out loud.

"I said, no, what *is* between you, Bob? I'd like to know."

"I would, too," my father added.

"If you two had a fight," I said, looking at both of them, "and I asked you what it was about you'd tell me to mind my own business."

"And that's what you're telling us?" my father asked.

I couldn't say that to my own father, so I shook my head. "There wasn't any fight and I just don't feel like talking about it," I said finally.

I quit jogging with them. I never liked to do it anyway. After a while, my father stopped, too.

# 21

May, June. The days got longer, too much longer for me. From our living room window I could see the dam at the end of the lake, where I used to watch for Brian those long-ago school mornings. Now what I saw was a gang. Sundback, Eugene, Kuhn, Brian, Neimeier, Gustafson—a couple, or three, or all of them, any given afternoon or evening—sitting on the wooden fence, or riding bikes up and down the road, or standing around in a clump.

I'd see them looking over at our house and if they thought I was watching they'd start throwing rocks at it. Of course, it was too far from the dam to our house for any of the rocks to hit, but they threw them anyway, laughing loudly when all the rocks landed with large splashes in the water.

One morning at the bus stop, I got a reprieve. Sundback was all excited about something and he had the other kids all worked up, too, telling them about it. I didn't find out till later what it was. All I could hear then, as I leaned up against the stone wall and tried to look inconspicuous, was some of the guys saying things like, "How about me" and "When can I" and "Boy, are you lucky, Emmett." Yeah, boy. Was Emmett Sundback lucky.

"You hear what I got, Chernowitz?" he said as he passed me in the hall, instead of his usual "C.K.C." or "Jew-boy."

"V.D.," I said.

"You're so smart, aren't you, Jew-boy?" he sneered. "Well, I got something just for you. My father gave me a motorcycle for my birthday and I'm going to use it to run you right over. Or maybe your cat."

I closed my eyes. You bastard, I thought.

He did have a motorcycle, he wasn't kidding. Of all the wrong people to have that kind of responsibility, Sundback was Number One.

My mother was the one who said that, actually, but she was right. He drove everybody crazy, riding back and forth across the dam, making so much noise you couldn't hear yourself think. Sound carries over water like you wouldn't believe! All the neighbors complained to each other but nobody did anything about it.

"I don't think it would do any good to call him," I overheard my mother saying to Mrs. Denny. "If the man gave him the thing in the first place . . . And the noise doesn't seem to bother him or he'd put a stop to it."

When she'd hung up I asked her what Mrs. Denny said.

"Well, she told me nobody wants to get involved with him," she answered, shrugging and shaking her head. "Mrs. Denny says they think he drinks."

"He's a lush?"

"I didn't say that, Bobby, but that's the impression Brian's mother gets from the neighbors."

Meanwhile, Sundback rode back and forth across the dam, up and down the road. Unless it was raining, he was always there when we had dinner which was a big drag, especially if we wanted to eat outside.

Finally, one day, my father'd had it. He walked over to the dam to talk to Sundback. I watched from the window, but it turned out there was nothing to see. As soon as Emmett saw my father coming toward him, he took off on that machine and he didn't come back. That evening, anyway.

After school, he started giving other kids rides on it or letting them ride it themselves. I wondered again about the Dennys because I knew Mrs. Denny had complained about the noise, but there was Brian, zooming around on the motorcycle, and I knew she could see him because their house faces the dam, too.

My father tried a couple more times to talk to Sundback, but each time he got near him, Sundback would ride away. So my father decided to call his father.

Which was not easy.

There was never any answer. Maybe that's why the bike didn't bother Mr. Sundback, he was never home!

Dad tried and tried.

"What kind of business can this man run?" he asked. "He doesn't even have an answering service to leave a message!"

One time Dad called when Emmett was not out tearing around on his bike and Emmett himself answered the phone.

"Is your father there?" Dad asked sternly. Then he made a face, cupped his hand over the mouthpiece and turned to Mom and me. "He says 'Who wants to know?' Young man, you put your father on this minute," he barked into the phone in his principal's voice. There was a pause. Then Dad said, "Now you look here: If another dinner of mine is ruined because of that damn machine of yours, your father *and* your mother *and* the school are going to hear about it. Is that understood?"

"What'd he say?" I asked when he was finished.

"Nothing. He just hung up."

Sundback stopped riding the bike during the dinner hour. Or at least, he stopped riding it over the dam. He'd ride it when Dad's car wasn't parked in front or he'd ride it at night, which made it awful hard to hear my Mets game but that didn't seem to bother Mom or Dad. Occasionally they'd make a disgusted face if the noise penetrated what they were doing, but that was about all.

It took me days and days to get up the nerve, but I finally decided to try something with Sundback. I kept thinking—if just the threat of going to his father or the school could make him quit that bikeriding, what if I tried a threat of my own? The thing that held me back so long was, I knew I'd never carry out the threat. I'd never go to his father. Or the school or his mother. I couldn't do it, it was too cowardly. And I'd have to live with it afterward, with the whole school knowing.

But if I just threatened? Would that have any effect on him? If I could threaten and not have to carry it out . . . If it worked, then maybe it was worth a try.

The next time he passed me, whispering "Jew," I stopped him. Not with my usual obscene remark, but by just saying his name.

"What, Jew-punk? What do you want?"

"I'm really getting tired of your stupidity," I said, trying to sound weary, "and I thought it was time I put a stop to it by having your father and Mr. Shafer and maybe a few people like that give you a little back. You think you'd like that, Sundback?" I looked away from him and began picking a hangnail to show how unconcerned I was with his answer. When I looked back, his face was actually scary.

"You ever tell anyone, Cherno, and I mean *anyone* . . . You won't even live to see the morning." Then he put his face right up close to mine. "No one would believe you, anyway," he said.

I wasn't afraid of him. I knew he wouldn't really hurt me, that wasn't his style. And I also knew that I would certainly be believed. None of that mattered. What mattered was I could never tattle on him. But he was afraid, there was no doubting that. He was so afraid that not only did he have to threaten me with my life, he also called me "Cherno" for the first time since the start of ninth grade.

# 22

At last—school ended.

I really welcomed exam week because everybody was too busy studying to pay much attention to me, all except for Sundback and his cousin, who probably didn't study at all. I hoped they both failed everything because in the fall I'd be in tenth grade and they'd still be in junior high—I'd never have to see them again for a whole year. Except on the bus . . .

I could tell that Sundback wanted me to cheat for him again in English, just by the way he kept trying to get my attention when we sat down. But I ignored him and the test was all essay anyway, so there wasn't much either of us could do about it even if I wanted to.

My overall average was ninety-two. Three points down from what it was in eighth grade. My parents could hardly complain about a ninety-two, but they muttered about the drop in points and my "attitude," which was becoming my mother's favorite word.

The soccer season ended with us finishing third,

but I'd really lost interest in it after the first coule of weeks. I thought if I played real well, it would be a way of maybe winning back Brian and Tim Kuhn, but even when I played fantastically it didn't work and after a while I stopped caring what they thought. It was all an act. They put one on for Sundback and then on the soccer field they put on one for their parents. But I did, too . . . So did I.

When the Mets didn't get any better, I decided that all the bad things in the world were happening to me, but that was okay because while other people spread out their troubles, I was getting all mine over with in one year and it would be smooth sailing from then on.

Right? . . .

# 23

We have a Sunfish. It's a little sailboat. My father bought it from the people who used to live in the Dennys' house, before they moved away. I guess they could have sold it to the Dennys but we were friends and we asked them when their house first went on the market. I used to take sailing lessons from a college kid who grew up on the lake and I enjoyed going out on it. Our association ran Sunfish races every weekend: Saturdays were for the "Juniors," the kids, and Sundays for the grownups. I never entered the races. Maybe that's another thing about me that wasn't "one of the boys," but I simply wasn't interested in the boat as a competitive thing. I just liked the feeling of skimming across the water, seeming to go much faster than you actually are, watching the tiny waves lick up the side of the boat, feeling like an extension of water, wind and sky. Competition—races— they were okay if that's what you liked, it just wasn't *my* thing.

The summer before ninth grade, I entered

some races with Brian because he wanted to. You're supposed to race with two, pilot and crew, and he and I took turns sailing and being the crew after I taught him how. We came in second once, the closest we ever came to winning. He was really hot on winning and I really wasn't, but I tried, to accommodate him. He didn't get how I felt about the boat but I understood how he felt about winning, so I worked at it for him. When the season ended, he said, "Next year we'll show 'em, Bobby, next year we'll sail the course during the week and practice and by the weekends we ought to be great!" I'd said, "Sure, we'll do that," figuring I'd still have lots of time for private sailing. It didn't hurt me to do the races, I just didn't think it was the point of having the boat.

This past summer, after my Sundback Year, I thought I'd have all the time I wanted for private sailing, but Denny's lack of loyalty faked me out again.

Right before the July Fourth weekend, Sundback went with his mother and his sister to visit relatives in Minnesota. I found that out when there was no motorcycle noise and no gang hanging around the dam. My mother remarked about the peace and quiet to some neighbor in the supermarket and that's what the neighbor told her. And with Sundback gone, the other kids just went on doing what they always did, swimming at the beach or playing tennis or whatever.

I went to the beach, too. It was a little private beach for the lake association families so it was never very crowded except on weekends, when the families brought their company and all their kids.

When I went down I'd see the people I always saw plus the summer people who rented houses on the lake every year. If Kuhn or Neimeier or Gustafson or any of those guys were around they left me alone; they didn't try the bus stop stuff on me and they didn't chant or anything or dunk me in the water. I was alone, but I didn't mind. It was a lot better than being picked on.

And I worked, too. I cut lawns. I took care of five lawns—including my own, which I didn't get paid for—and my customers kept me pretty busy. So I used sailing as my little reward when I was through work for the day.

We keep the boat right at our own dock in the back of our house. One day in July, while Sundback was still gone, I went down, rigged the sail, and went out. It was a calm day, no wind, but it was nice. I had on a swimsuit and figured I'd just get a tan, like the one I had in Florida.

The idea of a tan made me think of Matty Greeley, whom I hadn't said a word to besides "Hi" the rest of the school year. Once it had looked as if she were stopping to say more to me but I didn't give her a chance, I just walked off. All I could see was Sundback making a fool of me when I looked at Matty. But then, in the boat, I thought about calling her up. With Sundback gone and no school—

The sound of my name cut through my thoughts. I looked up. Brian Denny was floating by my boat on an inflated truck tire inner tube.

"Hey," he said. "How you doing?"

I couldn't believe it. That was really chutzpah! I didn't answer him and started to tack, but he paddled with his hands and caught up easily, since I needed a breeze to move and he didn't.

"You want to enter the Saturday race?" he asked, as if nothing at all had happened all year. I just stared at him.

"Hey, I said you wanna race Saturday?" he repeated, paddling all around my boat.

"What's the matter, can't you go with any of your friends?" I asked.

He didn't answer that and then I almost smiled as I remembered that Tim Kuhn always raced with Cliff Neimeier—they'd been together for years. And Gustafson and Levoy didn't sail. The other kids were either younger or older and he didn't know them that well anyway. So if Denny wanted to go sailing he'd either have to buy his own boat or use mine. That's why he was coming on.

"Denny," I said, "you're either short on brains or you've got nerve in your veins instead of blood. Paddle the hell out of here."

"Ah, come on, Cherno, can't you take a joke or anything? That's why you have such a bad time, you're so goddam serious. Neimeier says you were always like that."

He has nobody to hang around with and he can't stand it, I thought. Or he wants to sail worse than anything.

I leaned over and stared at him. "Calling somebody a Jew-bastard is a joke to you?" I said.

"Come on, it's just a word, it doesn't mean anything," he said with a wave of his fingers.

I started to go.

"It didn't mean anything!" he repeated. "What was I gonna call you, 'Mr. Too-Serious'? We were only teasing you . . ."

I didn't sail away from him but I tuned him out. Part of me wanted to say okay to him. Even though I'd never forget what he did, he obviously could. Maybe it really didn't mean something so ominous to him, even though it was ominous. And evil. But if I was the only one who thought so . . .

And if I made friends with him, then at least when he knew how I felt he'd never let something like that happen again . . .

I stared at the water. Brian had hurt me more than I even realized. I was thinking how much fun we'd had before, how convenient it was to have a friend living so close, how many fun things there were to do with someone else all summer . . . Overlooking not only how quickly he'd dropped me, but the horrible things he'd said, just to be a part of the gang.

Calling someone a name probably didn't have significance for him. He'd just go along with whatever the kids did, just so they'd like him.

And now there were no kids around, only me. That was Brian Denny. My friend.

"What do you say, Bobby, you wanna forget it?" he was saying as his tube bobbed up and down in the water.

"I can't forget it, Brian," I said quietly, but I still didn't sail the boat away.

After a minute, he slid off the tube and started swimming with it toward his house.

That night, he phoned me. My dad answered and came excitedly into the living room where I was watching the Mets.

"It's Brian Denny on the phone," he whispered.

"Huh?"

"I said it's Brian. For you!"

I sighed. My father looked so happy that Brian was making this kind move to end all our troubles. Dad was working so hard—he heads up a summer program at the community college and they don't have much in the way of funds, so he does most of the work—I just didn't have the heart to make him feel bad.

"Okay," I said, getting up. Dad winked at me and walked out of the kitchen to give me some privacy. Just what I needed with Brian Denny.

"Hey, Bobby, listen, just to show you there's no hard feelings . . ." he began. There were truckloads of hard feelings! "I thought I'd ask you first if you want to take over Jordy's paper route when we go on vacation in two weeks."

Brian's brother had the best paper route in the neighborhood. The kid was a little hustler and had sewn up practically every customer on three lake streets.

"Jordy wanted to ask Brandon Smith from his class, but I gave him fifty cents to ask you. I figured maybe it would square things, because I accidentally gave you a bad time."

I held the phone away from my ear. I really couldn't believe it.

"Bob?" he said. "Bob? You there?"

"Yeah . . ."

"He's got sixteen customers. And they're good tippers. You could make as much as you make cutting lawns. And it's easier. And quicker, too."

Sure. I'd take it. Why not?

"How long will you be on vacation?" I asked.

"Two weeks. We're going to Cape Cod."

Have a wonderful time. "Okay. Tell Jordy to get me a list of the people and what days they take the paper."

"Right. Hey—you're wel-come, Robert," he sang.

I hung up.

Both my parents looked expectantly at me as I came back into the living room.

"What happened?" I asked.

"Bottom of the fourth, still nothing-nothing. What did Brian want?" my father asked.

"Asked if I'd take Jordy's paper route while they went on vacation."

"Well, wasn't that nice?" my mother said. "You're doing it, aren't you? That'll be some good extra money you hadn't planned on."

"Yeah, I'm doing it."

"Well, wasn't it nice of Brian to think of you? I guess that's his way of saying he's sorry you had that fight."

"Yeah, that's his way," I answered.

# 24

The next couple of weeks were awkward as hell.

I had to take Brian out on the boat. I had to. His parents invited my parents—and me, too, of course—over for a barbecue in their back yard. There was no way I could stop that or get out of going.

I looked like the Rat of the Year for not participating joyously in the gala event. Everyone was laughing and cooking and throwing a beach ball around and swinging in the Dennys' hammock out over the water . . .

And there I was, sitting at the edge of the lawn, munching on what tasted like a cardboard hamburger and hating the weather for not having rained.

"Oh, come on, Bobby, don't sit like a lump. Here, have one of these," my mother would say, stuffing something into my mouth.

"Come on, Son, join us here," my father would call.

"Here, Bobby, give Bri and Jordy a hand with

this, won't you?" from one of the Dennys. Nobody would let me be.

"I've got an idea," my father said, after we'd eaten and they were sitting around the picnic table having coffee. "How about you boys taking the Sunfish out? Why, you haven't been in one race yet. With some practice, you can get one in before the Dennys leave."

"Great!" Brian cried. "Come on, Bob, let's swim over to your house and get the boat!"

So we did. I don't think Brian gave a damn about whether I was talking to him or not. Or maybe he was just too thick to notice. He was so glad to be out in that boat, he just kept jabbering the entire time we were out. "How do I do this, is this right? I forgot . . . Oh! Yeah, I remember, let me take it, let *me* . . ."

I didn't have to entertain him. But I did have to be there.

Finally, the Dennys went away. Jordy brought my list over the night before they left for the Cape. My hand shook when I saw the name "Albert Sundback" on it but then I remembered that Emmett was away, so that would be all right. All I had to do was deliver a lousy local paper, anyway, I didn't have to stay for tea!

# 25

Some woman in a brown station wagon dumped the papers near the Dennys' corner every afternoon at around two o'clock. My job was to see that they got to all the houses before five. On weekends it was a morning paper, though, and they had to be delivered before eight.

The extra job made me have to schedule my time, which I liked. The first day I did a lawn in the morning, took a swim, ate lunch and weeded our vegetable garden.

By the time I finished, the papers were dropped and I rode over on my bike to pick them up and deliver them early. That way I could get another lawn done in the afternoon and then swim till supper.

I was riding on Daley Lane, past the hedges near the Sundback property. I would have known it was Sundback's anyway, even if the name hadn't been out front, because there were stacks of new and used lumber all over the place. Anyway, I was riding by his hedges, when all of a sudden a stick shot out from them and caught my wheel spokes. The bike jammed and I went over, flailing around, trying to regain my balance. It was no use. I landed smack against the hedges and it really hurt since all I was wearing was a pair of shorts, not even a shirt. I got scratched up pretty badly, and while I was looking myself over kind of shakily, a blond head popped up over the top of the hedges.

"Miss me, Chernowitz?" Sundback asked, beaming at me.

Something really snapped inside and I ran around the hedge toward him. All I could think of was choking him to death. I saw he was in a bathing suit and there was a garden hose on the lawn that the water was running out of. Since he looked wet, I guessed he'd been hosing himself down to get cool, and he felt awfully slippery as I grabbed him.

We started wrestling but I knew I was no match for him. Not only was he bigger and heavier, but wrestling was his school sport besides. So I tried to get back so I could punch him. I think I was crying, too, but it was because I was so mad. The scratches didn't even hurt, it felt so good to grab, pinch, hit—anything that would cause Emmett Sundback pain.

I tried, I really did. I used everything my father had ever taught me plus a few things of my own, including dirty fighting; but he outweighed me by so much and he really did know how to fight, I could tell.

He finally backed me up against a pile of wood

with such force that I knocked over almost the whole top layer.

When that happened, Albert Sundback, Emmett's father, came out of his garage. He was an even bigger version of Emmett only he'd lost most of his black curly hair.

"What the hell you doing?" he bellowed. "Get the hell away from my wood! Who the hell you think you are!"

Emmett straightened up quickly. "It wasn't me, Pop, *he* did it!"

I stared at both of them.

"He did it, Pop, he was foolin' around near the wood. I was tryin' to get him away, honest!"

"Get the hell off my property!" Emmett's father roared at me.

I decided he was drunk. He looked like he was reeling, though I probably was, too, right then.

Emmett wasn't looking at me. I don't think I even existed for him any more. He was watching to see what his father was going to do next.

I didn't run away. I was not afraid of Mr. Sundback and not even of Emmett then. So I took my time walking around to my bike and picking up the rest of my papers.

Some of my scratches were bleeding a little, but the thing that hurt the most was my shoulder, where Emmett had knocked me back against the wood.

I moved around a little, making sure all the parts of my body were still working. They were. And then I remembered, I still hadn't delivered the paper. I walked over the opening in the hedge. Mr. Sundback had gone back into the garage. I could hear him moving stuff inside. Emmett was just standing there rubbing his elbow.

"Hey, Sundback," I said. He turned. "Here's your paper." I flung it at him, hitting his leg. He made as if to come after me, then turned toward the house to see if anyone were watching. I left then . . .

I rode my bike back to the Dennys', walked around the side of their house to the lake and carefully slid off the grassy bank into the water. That move was mainly to clean myself up, but it felt so cool and beautiful I just floated around, I don't even know for how long.

When I got home, I put a shirt on right away to hide the scratches.

# 26

Emmett Sundback was home from vacation and there were the kids hanging around the dam again and there was the unmuffled motorcycle speeding around the back roads. When I went down to the beach there were remarks made, once again, but not loud enough for anyone but me to hear. Once, when I was lying on my towel on the sand, Neimeier came up and dumped a bucket of water over me. I had a book and a watch and everything and all of it got soaked. Everyone laughed, but when I jumped up and chased Neimeier into the water and dunked his head under, they didn't laugh any more. They yelled, "Ah, Cherno can't even take a joke!" and the lifeguard called me out of the water for dunking, which is against the rules.

But I wouldn't let them force me away from the beach or any place else. I still went down when I felt like it. I wondered what would happen when the Dennys came home and Sundback got to Brian again.

I kept delivering the papers. Once Sundback

turned the hose on me but nothing much worse
than that. I guessed his father was hanging
around.

When it came time to collect for the papers
the first week, I knocked on Sundback's door. I
was nervous but not afraid. I think that was
because I knew I had no choice; I had to collect,
somebody was going to answer that door, and I
had to deal with it one way or another.

Emmett's father answered. He looked down
at me blankly. I guessed he'd forgotten about
yelling at me. Or maybe he was drunk like the
neighbors were saying.

He said. "Heh?"

"I'm here to collect for the Middleboro News,
Mr. Sundback," I said politely.

"You?" he said.

"Yes . . ."

"You grew since the last time you collected,
kid," he said and chuckled to himself. I figured
that was supposed to be a joke referring to little
Jordy.

"Jordy Denny is on vacation," I said, "so I'm
doing it for him this week and next."

"Ah-*hah*," he said, acknowledging that. "Al-
right, wait here a minute."

He closed the screen door and went away. I
played this silly kid-game while he was getting
the money: If he comes back before I count to
ten slowly then I won't see Emmett . . .

He did and I didn't see Emmett.

"Still two dollars, right?" he asked, handing
me two ones.

"Still two," I said, pocketing them. No tip. It was okay. I figured my tip was not being hassled. I raced for my bike with my heart pounding. I was more scared than I'd told myself.

"Hey, kid!" I heard from the door. I whirled around.

"Get you next time!" Mr. Sundback called.

"What?" I called back. My voice was hoarse.

"Next time!" he yelled again. "A tip! I got no change now!"

I almost fell down with relief. "Oh! Yeah, right!" I answered, swinging my leg over the bike bar. "Don't worry about it!" Don't worry about it, I repeated to myself as I rode away.

I didn't know what I'd expected, but Mr. Sundback hadn't seemed like what I thought Emmett's father would be if I ever had to face him. He was just a guy, that was all. Just a guy . . .

The next week—the last time I was to collect for Jordy—Emmett was there to pay me.

"There's a tip in there for you, paperboy. Better late than never," he said, and he closed the door.

I knew it had to be something really rotten or Emmett never would have closed the door and let it speak for itself!

I was right. On a piece of paper he had made the sign of the Nazis, the swastika, drawn in black crayon.

That sign. That dreaded and dreadful sign . . . Six million Jews died under that sign be-

cause an insane bully had an insane idea. Six
million people tortured.

I started to shiver. I thought of the note in
English class. This must be what Mr. Shafer had
seen and ripped up, and given us a test for.
"Better late than never . . ." Emmett had said.

There had been such terror behind that sign . . .

And Emmett knew it, too. He probably flunked
history, but he knew about the swastika.

I had crumpled the paper without even realiz-
ing it. Now I opened it and smoothed it. I didn't
show it to anyone, but I kept it. My "tip."

Three days later, Brian and his family came
back.

# 27

I was never sure what did happen with Brian. All I knew was it was his turn to feel awkward then and I could see it. My parents invited the Dennys to a barbecue to pay them back for theirs and Brian came, but he wasn't so peppy and nice to me, like before. Now it was his turn to sulk in the corner of the deck. I sure didn't help him out any, and the afternoon was spent with the parents trying to talk us both into "doing something together." When they hit on the Sunfish both of us went out, but Brian sailed and I just crewed and neither of us talked.

I'd see him with the gang on the dam in the evenings and I'd see him riding around on Sundback's motorcycle, too. So now he had the motorcycle back to play with; that was faster than a Sunfish any old day!

Even though Sundback was around, even though Brian was what he was, even though the kids I grew up with were all different toward me—and even though the Mets were losing everything!—I still didn't have a bad summer. It wasn't great, but it wasn't bad.

I made money through my own hard work and not from an allowance and that felt good. I loved the weather, the feel of the sun and all the smells you smell in summer, especially when you're cutting a lawn. But best of all, I didn't feel afraid any more. It was like Sundback was there, he was part of my life all right, but he didn't affect every waking minute of it, like he used to at school. It's like you're subject to migraine headaches, and when you get one it's just awful, but you can't wake up every day worrying about whether you're going to get one or not. It's a possibility, but you have other stuff to think about.

One of the things I liked to think about was Matty Greeley. I hadn't seen her all summer, not even once, but I made up all kinds of nice things about her in my head and she was a lot better to think about than Emmett Sundback.

My father's summer job ended about ten days before Labor Day weekend and the beginning of school. Every year we talked about going away for that time, but we rarely did. Even though practically everyone on the lake went away in the summertime, we always felt that our vacation was right here and we loved it. Everything you go away in the summer for is right here— water sports of all kinds and a real country feeling. Summer doesn't last all that long, either, so we like to just hang around the house and enjoy it.

Sometimes we went sailing, the three of us. They were silly times because it's a two-man boat and one of us was always falling in.

I remember that whole week was beautiful. It didn't rain once, and we ate every meal outside, even breakfast. Dad would cook eggs on the gas grill while Mom and I would take a quick swim or feed the ducks or something.

One morning in particular . . . I had such a feeling of peace it made me realize how long it had been since I'd had the feeling. I thought of Florida and how good it had been down there, away from everything . . .

I was lying on the deck on a towel, drying off after a swim. Dad was frying eggs and Mom had just brought out the coffee. Nasty Cat was curled up on the chaise, which was why I was on the floor. The air smelled good . . .

"Jerry?" my mother said, sitting down at the picnic table. "Remember how your father loved mornings like this out here?"

My father smiled. "He really did, didn't he? He loved this place . . ."

"He used to bring out his books, remember? All those books and newspapers . . ."

My father laughed. "His *Daily Forwards*. All those *Daily Forwards* he saved because he never got a chance to read them during the week . . ."

"Months!" my mother cried. "He had *months* of *Forwards!*"

My father laughed again. "He said the English newspapers were harder for him to read, so he concentrated on them every night. The *Forwards* were his 'relaxation,' so he saved them for weekends and vacations."

"I remember them," I said. "The Jewish newspapers. You couldn't read them, could you, Dad?"

"No, not really," my father answered. "I learned what I needed to know for my Bar Mitzvah, but I was never much interested . . ."

"I don't think the English papers were hard for him to read," my mother said dreamily, looking out over the lake. "I think he just bought those *Forwards* to touch base with his roots. You know?

"He never really read them. He just dragged them out here on the deck with all the books he never read either . . . He must have sat out here and stared at the water . . . for hours . . ."

"Yeah . . . his roots," my father repeated. "They're always there for you, whether or not there's an outward show of remembering. It's not the 'show' that's important anyway . . ."

I listened to them and I thought about Emmett Sundback. Not in a fearful way just then, but in kind of a dreamy way. I wondered just what he would think if he could hear my parents talking together about my grandfather and his Jewish newspapers and his roots. I thought how far away from a conversation like this he was . . .

"Rae?" I heard my father say softly.

"Yes, Jerry?"

"I just burned the eggs."

We had a wonderful week of relaxation together as a family when it suddenly all blew up.

\*     \*     \*

Sundback is not what you'd call subtle. I knew something was weird even days before it happened. The kids started hanging around near our house instead of at the dam. Not on our property, but right next to it on the association's property. And they'd start laughing and whispering, just like they had on Halloween. I figured Sundback was planning something, I just didn't know what.

And one morning, early, before any of us were up, there was a knock on the door. My father heard it upstairs; he's a light sleeper. I heard him creep past my room and so I got up and followed him. When he opened the front door, there was Mr. Denny in shorts and a hooded sweatshirt.

"Sorry to wake you up, Jerry," I heard him say. "I know you're on vacation . . ."

"What's wrong, Charlie?"

"I was jogging past here . . . I didn't see it first time around because it was on the other side, but coming back, it sure hit me right in the face—"

"What are you talking about, Charlie?" my father repeated.

"Uh . . . I guess maybe you better come on out and see it for yourself," Mr. Denny said.

I had been sleeping in my underpants, so I quickly ran back into my room to throw on a pair of shorts. My father went right out in his pajamas.

I could hear my mother moving around in their bedroom as I tore downstairs. Outside, my father and Mr. Denny were standing at the top of our hill in the parking area looking at my mother's car. I raced up there.

Neither of them was speaking and I could see why. On the side of my mother's light blue Chevy, someone had painted a huge swastika. It covered practically the whole side of the car, from the top to the bottom, even over the windows. Someone had used shiny black paint that was still dripping. Someone.

Mr. Denny was shaking his head. "Jeez, Jerry, who'd do something like that?" he whispered, but my father didn't answer. He was just staring at it.

"What is it, Jerry?" my mother called from the front door. "Jerry?"

When he didn't answer, she disappeared into the house to throw a robe on over her nightgown. Soon she was beside us and I heard her gasp.

"Oh, Jerry!"

"Listen, let me help you wash it off, Jer," Mr. Denny said. But my father still didn't answer. My mother stood there with her hand covering her mouth.

I turned back into the house and was sick in the bathroom.

A few minutes later we were alone in the house. Mr. Denny had jogged home to get some paint remover. My parents and I sat down heavily in the living room; each of us was shivering.

"Do you have any idea who would do such a

thing?" my mother almost whispered and my father shook his head.

"Do you, Bobby?" he asked, turning to me. "Do you know any kids who would? It has to be kids . . . Bob, do you think the Sundback kid—? The one who picked on you back last fall—?"

I licked my lips.

"Bobby?"

"It was Sundback," I said. "I know it was. He never quit picking on me. He's just—he's a bully. A torturer, that's what he is . . . He likes to make people afraid. He likes to make them smaller than he is. And he can do it, he's done it. Stay here a minute . . ." I ran up the stairs to my room and over to my dresser. In the top drawer under my socks was where I kept my "tip" from the newspapers. I brought down the crumpled paper and handed it to my father. I saw him look at it, close his eyes and pass it to my mother.

"When did he give this to you?" my father asked softly.

"It was a 'tip' for the newsboy. When I was delivering the Middleboro News. He made that drawing for me once before, in English, only Mr. Shafer got it first and tore it up before I could see it. I never did know what was on that note until Sundback gave me this one. He said 'Better late than never' and I'm sure that's what he meant."

"Aaron Shafer tore it up?" my mother asked.

"Yeah, I guess it made him sick," I said.

"Well, what did he do? Did he know who sent it? Did he know it was for you?"

"No, nobody would tell, are you kidding? He just gave us a test in the middle of the period."

My mother sighed. "What else?" she asked.

I hesitated. I couldn't tell them about Kuhn, Neimeier . . . Brian Denny. I just couldn't. These people were their friends, their neighbors for years. How would they look at them after this if they knew what their kids had done . . . and said . . .

"Sundback didn't beat me up or anything like that," I said. "He never did anything like that," I said. "He never did anything where adults could see him, he'd just pass remarks. In the halls, in English, anywhere he saw me . . ."

My mother had her hand over her mouth. "I don't understand why you never told us," she said through her fingers.

"I didn't want to involve you," I murmured.

"In*volve* us! Oh, Bobby, we're your parents! We're *supposed* to be involved!"

"No, you don't understand," was all I could manage.

"But you lived with this—all this time—all by yourself!" My mother was crying.

"I should have made you take karate lessons," my father said, smacking his fist against his palm. "You should have showed that kid what for long ago. I'm going over there to his father now and—"

"That's *it*, Dad, that's what I mean!" I interrupted sharply. "I didn't want you in it! It's *me*, not you! I wanted to handle it!"

"But it's not just you, don't you see?" my

father protested. "It's all of us!" He ground his teeth. "I'd like to kill the little anti-Semite—"

"Oh, Dad, wait—" I managed at the same time my mother said, "Just a minute, Jerry, let's talk this out," and in the middle of all of us talking at the same time, there was a knock at the screen door.

"Jerry?" Mr. Denny called out. "Jerry, I've got something here to get the paint off . . . Are you guys ready? Come on, let's get that thing off!"

My mother stood up. Her face was white, the color of her cotton robe. "Don't wash it off, Jerry," she whispered.

"What?"

"Don't wash the—the thing off."

"Rae, are you crazy?"

"No, I mean it. That's what happened in Nazi Germany, nobody said anything, everybody swept it all under the rug, *it can't happen here*, remember? Leave it there! Leave it there and call the Middleboro News! Tell them to come over and take a picture of . . . of a local happening!"

"Rae, what do you—"

"Tell them to put a picture of our car in the paper. Show the whole town!"

My father shook his head, misunderstanding. "Honey, I don't think we can accuse the kid in the paper without positive proof."

"We won't accuse him. It's not to accuse him, don't you see? It's to show that it happened here in our town. Let everybody see. Maybe they'll

be appalled enough to remember—to watch what
their kids do. This kid knows what he did, he'll
see the picture in the paper, that'll be enough.
But don't hide this—"

"Hey, Jerry!" Mr. Denny called again. "You
coming out? I've started!"

"Wait! Wait, Charlie!" my mother called,
hurrying to the door. "Jerry, it's more effective
than having Bobby beat a kid. It would have
been better if Aaron Shafer had shown the whole
class that note instead of tearing it up! Jerry,
call the paper!"

The Middleboro News sent a photographer
and a reporter. We told them we had a fair idea
of the person responsible but we weren't saying
anything yet. They took a picture and then the
four of us—Mr. Denny, my parents and I—
scrubbed the swastika off our car.

"Who was it, Jerry?" Mr. Denny asked when
we were through.

My father started to answer him, but I interrupted.

"We'd really rather not say right now, Mr.
Denny," I said. "This is a family problem."

My father looked at me questioningly but I just
shook my head. For all I knew, Brian Denny
could have been one of them.

# 28

The picture was printed two days later and our phone started ringing like crazy.

My mother smiled for the first time since it happened.

"See?" she said. "The neighbors are being wonderful. I just knew it was right to broadcast that horrible thing . . . It only gets worse if you try to sweep it under the rug like you're embarrassed about it!"

"Maybe you're right," my father said. "Maybe it was the thing to do. But now that it's out, I want to go over to that Sundback kid's house and talk to his father."

My heart sank.

"Oh, Dad, don't do that, don't do it," I wailed. "It won't solve anything, really, it won't!"

But he took my shoulders in his hands. "Look, Bob, I've got to do this. I didn't go over there hotheaded two days ago. I'm still hotheaded, I have to admit, but I've done a lot of thinking. Now what you have with this kid is bad enough,

117

but it's gone beyond that. And you will agree that it's family property that's been defaced."

"Jerry . . . The man drinks," my mother said weakly.

"Now don't you start, too, Rae . . ."

"No, no, I think he should be spoken to, only just . . . I don't know, be careful, I guess."

"I'm only going to talk, Rae," my father said.

"I'm going, too," I said miserably.

"No, Bobby!" my mother cried, but my father nodded.

"I think he should go," he said. "I think it's right that he be there, Rae." He touched my shoulder again.

I never thought I'd be knocking at the Sundbacks' door another time for any reason, but there we were, my father and I, standing out there as the sky was turning purple, and all I could think of was how unpeaceful I felt in this peaceful setting.

The door was yanked open by Emmett whose face crumpled up the second he saw Dad and me on his front step.

"Get your father," was all Dad said.

Emmett got it together enough for an arrogant-sounding yell toward his basement door. He didn't ask us in, but stood there looking at everything and anything but us until Mr. Sundback could be heard clumping up the basement steps.

"Yeh?" he said gruffly, just as he had when I collected my two dollars for the paper.

"May we come in for a few minutes, Mr.

Sundback?" my father asked. "I'd like to talk to you and—" he nodded toward Emmett "—your son."

"Oh, yeh?" Mr. Sundback frowned in Emmett's direction. "A-right. Come in." Both he and Emmett backed out of the way as we stepped inside.

Mr. Sundback led us into the living room. It smelled musty. The furniture was a mixture of real old upholstered stuff and modern things, the kind of furniture you see in some motel lobbies. I figured he'd thrown together whatever he could when he moved into this house he'd built.

I sat next to Dad on the couch. Mr. Sundback sat in an old armchair. Emmett stood.

That was the last quiet moment.

"Mr. Sundback, my son, Bob, and I are here to talk to you about your boy, Emmett—his behavior toward my son and toward our family."

Mr. Sundback leaned back in his chair.

Dad started talking sitting down, but he didn't stay sitting down long. I saw he was trying to hold himself together, but the more into the story he got, about Emmett and the remarks he'd made and the things he did in English, the swastika note—the louder he got. He began to pace.

"And it isn't only *our* peace he disturbed," my father said, rubbing his knuckles into his palm. "That damn motorcycle you got him drove the whole neighborhood crazy all summer, going over and over the dam, especially at dinner time, nobody could hear himself *think—*"

Mr. Sundback stood up then, too. "Listen, Mr.—" he began, but Dad cut him off.

"But the topper, Mr. Sundback, I've saved this part for last—was the damage he did to my car two mornings ago. You did read about it in the paper, didn't you? Didn't you?"

Mr. Sundback looked over at Emmett, who wasn't looking at anybody.

"He's crazy, Pop," Emmett said quietly, shaking his head. "That wasn't me, he's crazy. I never did any of that stuff. He's been out to get me in trouble, I swear."

"He says he didn't do it," Mr. Sundback said. "You got any proof he did it?"

My father took Emmett's swastika out of his pocket and handed it to Mr. Sundback. "This is what he gave Bob for the papers as a 'tip.' "

Mr. Sundback looked at the paper. "This don't prove anything," he said.

"He made it himself," Emmett said. "He did it to get me in trouble. I didn't do none of it."

"You didn't even look at the note," I said to Emmett. It was the first time I'd spoken.

"I don't have to," he said, narrowing his eyes. It was a threat, I knew it. I knew this whole visit was a mistake.

"Listen." Mr. Sundback walked toward the entrance to the living room. "Emmett says he didn't do those things. You walk in my house and you start accusing here. Nobody else ever said anything about him, hear? Not about the motorcycle bothering them or anything. So you can just take your accusations and you can walk right out of here."

I looked at Emmett, knowing I'd see a big sneer on his face, but there wasn't any. Emmett just looked as upset as I know I looked.

My father and I followed Mr. Sundback to the front door.

"Mr. Sundback," my father said, "I know that Bob and I just stormed over here and upset your evening with a lot of accusations about your son."

"You bet you did," Mr. Sundback said.

"But I wouldn't have done that if I weren't sure of what I was saying. You talk to him. You know your boy. You see if what I'm telling you isn't true. And Mr. Sundback, I want this to be the end of any contact Emmett has with my son. Please understand that."

As Dad and I walked home without a word, I kept thinking of why Emmett hadn't looked smug while his father was defending him.

My mother was waiting at the door when we got home. She must have watched for us coming over the dam in the moonlight.

"What happened?" she asked quickly.

My father smiled slightly. "We're all in one piece," he said. "No blows exchanged."

"Tell me, Jerry!"

"All right, all right, Rae. I accused, Emmett denied, the father defended. I didn't expect much more, but I let the father know what had happened and that I didn't expect that anything more *would* happen."

"Didn't he even question Emmett in front of you?"

"No, I guess I didn't think he would, not after what we've heard about the guy, as little as it is. I just made my point. I hope it dies there. Do you feel a little better, Bob?"

I sighed. "I don't know," I said. "Mr. Sundback seemed okay enough the day I collected from him, but I'm not sure I feel better after tonight . . ."

"Well, I think you can," my father said. "I don't think Emmett will want us over there again."

"Why not, his father stuck up for him," I said.

"In front of us, yes. But I don't think he'll want any more trouble, either. After all, he does earn his living here. He does have to maintain some kind of reputation."

"Maybe," my mother interjected, "maybe we should talk to Sylvia before school starts."

"Sylvia?" I asked, panicking again. "You mean the high school principal?"

"Mrs. Wardwell. Yes."

"No, Mom, don't do that!" How many times had I said that in the last few days. "Please don't talk to Mrs. Wardwell. Look, you talked to the Sundbacks, now let it go, see what happens. Please. We can't prove anything, remember, and I have to live at that school every day, you don't!"

"All right," my father said. "Let's just see what happens."

# 29

On Labor Day, the lake association had a picnic on the beach for its members. My parents were anxious to go so we went. I had a feeling that Emmett and his father wouldn't be there and they weren't. Someone told my father it was because they hadn't paid their dues but my father hoped it was because Emmett was embarrassed. I just didn't think a picnic on the beach with a bunch of families was a thing Emmett would go to.

The picnic was pretty uneventful. Brian went out on Tim Kuhn's Sunfish so I didn't see much of either of them. I swam a lot of laps, played one game of water polo, ate hotdogs . . .

It was all right.

The next day, Tuesday, was sunny. And hot, like mid-August. Not the best weather for starting school the next day.

At least, for me. Dad had to go in to his school all day for teachers' meetings and last minute stuff. I decided to take advantage of the last of summer by spending the whole day at the beach. I took my lunch, a book and three magazines. Hardly anyone was there . . . The lifeguard finished working on Labor Day, and with no lifeguard the mothers didn't want to send their kids down alone.

It was nice . . . I thought about Matty Greeley . . . I hoped you could still get as tan from a September sun as from July and August . . .

I got back to the house at around four-thirty. My mother's car was gone, which surprised me a little since she said she'd be home all day, lazing around doing needlepoint on the deck.

I took a shower, put on some shorts and a shirt and just as I was coming back downstairs, Mom burst in through the screen door. Her face was red, but not from sunburn and she looked really upset.

"What happened?" I asked, stopping dead on the stairs.

"Oh," she said wiping her forehead with the back of her hand, "it's all right. It's going to be all right . . . I have to sit down, Bobby . . ."

"What *happened?*" I asked again, following her into the living room where she flopped heavily onto the couch.

"I just got back from taking Nasty to the vet. I was really scared for a little while. You should have seen me driving along Spring Street, it's a miracle I didn't get stopped . . ."

"Mom," I said, sitting down next to her, "what happened to Nasty?"

"I don't know, I don't know," she said. "I

guess he must have gotten sideswiped by a car or something. All I know is, I was on the deck doing my needlepoint and I felt thirsty, so I got up and was on my way into the kitchen, when I happened to glance out the screen door at the front steps. Well, my heart just stopped—there was poor Nasty, dragging—literally, Bobby— dragging his poor body down those steps toward me, toward the house. He was covered with blood, his back leg looked like—oh—" She shook her head and covered her eyes. "Well . . . of course I thought 'this is it,' you know, but I raced for the linen closet, grabbed a blanket and the car keys and just . . . just picked him up and got out of here!"

"But you said it's all right? He's going to be all right?"

"Yes," she said with a deep sigh. "His leg is broken, so it'll be in a cast for a while and he was bleeding from some minor cuts . . . I guess some flying stones hit him or something. But it didn't turn out to be as bad as it looked. That's the point. *I'm* the one still in cardiac arrest, the cat's going to be fine."

"Well, that's a relief," I said. "Where is he, still at the vet's?"

"Yes, we decided it would be better to let them watch him overnight, just to make sure everything's really all right. I'm supposed to get him tomorrow morning."

"Sorry I wasn't here," I said, "to help you."

"Oh, honey . . ." She patted my hand. "That's okay, I didn't even think. I just acted. The cars

race around here, especially in the summer . . .
It's awful on these back roads . . ."

"Are you okay now?" I asked.

"Sure. I'm okay. Look, it's lucky it wasn't a
child who was hit," she said.

Some last vacation day!

# 30

The next day, Wednesday, school began. Brian left early for the bus stop, just as he had last spring. So that hadn't changed.

This time I didn't dread the bus or school or anything. I was feeling all right about myself, about things, and so instead of timing my arrival at the bus stop with the bus's itself, I got there a little early.

There was the group—now tenth graders, although I had heard that Sundback had to take English and Science over again. They were standing together—Sundback, Neimeier, Levoy, Gustafson, Denny, Kuhn.

"And here he is . . . to make the little group complete," Sundback sang out. He didn't say "Chernowitz"; he didn't say "C.K.C."; he didn't say "Jew-bastard." Not yet. I waited.

"He has no hat, he has no books," he went on. "What can we steal off the you-know-what, boys?"

They all started to smile, including Brian. But one strange thing happened. Tim Kuhn moved away from the group. He did it so slowly, I hardly noticed it, but then I saw it was a definite move away. He didn't say anything, he didn't put anyone down, but suddenly, there he was, standing with some eleventh and twelfth graders, about as far away from Sundback's gang as you could get and still be at the same bus stop.

When the bus came, I got on it with the older group. I wanted to see if Kuhn would say something to me. Anything. He didn't. He just stayed away from Sundback.

When I got off the bus, Sundback was standing there, not walking toward the door like all the other kids. He was just standing, digging his toe in the grass, not even looking at me. As I walked past him, I heard his voice. It was low and hissy and it chilled me. He said three words. He said, "How's your kitty?"

I stopped. I felt like someone hit me in the stomach. Turning around slowly, I said, "What?"

He was smiling. "I said, 'How's your kitty?' Is it dead?"

I can't describe the feelings that went through me when Sundback said those three words to me. One thing I didn't do was turn around to question him any further. I kept right on going. I was ready to kill him right then, but some part of what I was feeling was such pure rage that I knew I'd have to think before I did anything else.

It wasn't a car, it was Sundback and his motorcycle. Sundback tried to kill Nasty with his motorcycle. I knew that now. I recalled he'd

even threatened to do it once. That was how
Nasty got hurt, it was Sundback!

This time I'd get him. This time I'd make him
pay, and I wouldn't use my father or my mother,
oh, no, not this time. I was going to get him.
Now it was Emmett Sundback's turn to watch
out.

# 31

One thing I did let my father do: arrange with the principal, Mrs. Wardwell, to see that I didn't have any classes with Sundback. And I asked my father not to tell her why. All I could do was hope that he respected my wish.

That meant that except for the bus ride, I didn't have to see Sundback at all. That is, he didn't have to *know* I was seeing him.

An idea began to take shape, and the more I thought of it, the more I liked it.

I played detective. I dogged him. The only period we had together was lunch. After lunch he'd leave early to go back to the junior high to repeat one of the two courses he flunked. He cooled it slightly toward me after the business with the cat, which I figured was to pay me back for that night at his house with my father. But we weren't thrown together as much as last year and I was sure he had no idea that I was planning a real revenge of my own.

Meanwhile, one nice thing happened. I discovered I had a study hall with Matty Greeley. She gave me such a big smile the first time we met in it that I knew it was a good omen and that everything was going to work out. Ninth grade had been bad, but like I had thought—I got all that over with and it was going to be fine from now on.

"How are things with the Sundback boy?" my mother asked. She asked it a lot in September.
"All right . . ."
"I think your father was right in wanting to tell the principal."
"Please, Mom. You promised."
"I didn't promise. I just didn't fight you."
"It'll be all right," I said. "I'm handling things."
By the end of October she quit asking.

Halloween this time was uneventful, although my father and I did our "raking bit" until eleven-thirty again. No one came to our house over the age of thirteen. My father and mother went peacefully to bed. In the morning we found shaving cream on our outdoor lantern and all over our cars, but everyone else on the street had the same thing.

Meanwhile I was learning about Sundback. One night I left the library early and sneaked around the back of his house. I was scared, but part of my plan was to learn as much about that weasel as I could. I hid behind a stack of two-by-fours that were piled under a lighted window. There was paper between the boards, the kind you see in lumber yards, and I folded it back carefully so that it wouldn't crinkle and I'd be able to lean against the wood and listen to whatever I could get.

What I heard was Sundback getting smacked around inside his house. I could actually hear the blows, that's how hard they were, and I could also hear him yelping. Like a dog. I wish I could say that it made me feel bad to hear him getting beaten like that but it didn't. I enjoyed it. I thought of Mom and Dad and Nasty and me and I enjoyed it.

And I also knew that he didn't need me to take karate lessons and beat him up. His father took care of that. He needed something different from me.

I crouched there a while after the noises stopped. I looked at the wood and its protective paper. Very quietly, a tiny bit at a time, I tore a chunk of the paper off, rolled it up and took it home with me.

Emmett's mother worked in an office down county. She was a quiet woman and so was the sister. Neither of them could handle Emmett and that's why they sent him to his father. For discipline. He got plenty of it. I learned about that from a gossipy lady at the town hall. She didn't mention any names but when I told her I was doing a project on the growth of the divorce rate in Middleboro, she came out with a lot of stuff. I didn't need or want any of it, but I knew when she was talking about the Sundbacks and that I listened to hard.

I found out his schedule and memorized it. I also knew which classes he liked to cut, which ones he'd always be late for, where he hung out in between, which days he had wrestling after school. If you're going to get revenge the right way, it takes a lot of planning.

He still hung around mostly with his cousin Eugene. He was with the lake kids some of the time but not as much as when they all stuck together against me. Except for Tim Kuhn. I never saw Sundback with Tim Kuhn again.

Anyway, I had the feeling that the only one he could really count on was Eugene, that his "lake gang" wasn't strong enough to back him up in any situation. All of that was good.

The most important information of all took me a month to get: Sundback's locker combination. I knew the locker number was B-203 and it was on the second floor across from the Home Ec room, but I needed that combination badly. I knew when he used the locker and I tried hanging out in the Home Ec room to see if I could catch any numbers at all. It was hard because I was too far away and I didn't want him to see me. Once I took a big chance and crept right up behind him while he was turning the dial, but all I saw was the first number and even then I couldn't be sure if it was a 16 or 17. I kept at it for weeks without any success and finally I knew that if I was going to get those numbers, I'd have to sneak them out of the school records.

I didn't want to do that. I hated the idea of it. I spent three whole nights trying all the possible

ways to get that locker combination without
prying into school files.

My parents noticed that I seemed "far away"
and asked me about it, but I assured them I was
really okay. I was. I was moving.

I decided that using another kid to act as a
diversion near the locker was totally out. There
was no way *anyone* besides me would become
involved.

That left only one real way. It would be a
little dangerous but I felt confident I could carry
it off.

The first thing I did was go into the office and
tell the secretary I lost the combination of my
own lock. That was just to see which file cabinet
she'd go to in order to look it up, and also where
she got the key to it.

That part was the easiest. The cabinet wasn't
even locked. Probably they left it unlocked during the day for easy access, because they were
lockable cabinets, I saw that.

I checked the cabinet, the drawer and even
how she looked through it to get to my number.
No problem. But getting into that drawer by
myself was something else.

It had to be at a time when both secretaries
were out of the office. One or the other of them
was going in or out all the time, but to get both
of them out of there at once was a real trick.

I hung around out in the hall for days, watching the office through its glass windows. The
only time both of them were away from their

desks I was too scared to try anything. I didn't
know how long they'd be gone.

I decided I'd have to give myself a little
insurance, I just couldn't leave it to chance.

It happened just before Thanksgiving. We'd
had an early snow. It wasn't a bad storm or
anything, but every time there's even a little
snow in Middleboro, things get started late. It is
country, kind of, and the teachers have to watch
the ice on those back roads.

I ran down to the office as soon as I could get
a pass out of Science, just to see if the secretaries made it in, and one of them hadn't! At least,
not yet. There was only one coat hung up on the
coat rack in the corner!

I went down the hall quickly and slipped into
the library. No librarian at the desk! Everything perfect. I pressed the button on the inter-
com and called the main office.

"Mrs. Kinney?" I said, just to double check.

"No, Mrs. Kinney won't be in until this afternoon. This is Mrs. Wersky, may I help you?"

"Yeah," I said, "this is Room 210. My teacher
asked me to call. He's here, but there's a substitute who says she was called for our class.
Anyway, could you come up here for a second
and straighten it out?"

"What room, did you say?"

"210."

"Mr. Van Ness?"

"Right."

"Well, I know he's here. What's the substitute's
name?"

"Uh . . . Well . . . I don't know, see, they just stepped out in the hall . . ."

"Never mind," she said, "I'll be right there."

Those words were my "insurance."

She passed me in the hall. I'd sent her upstairs to the farthest room. I had perhaps ten minutes, but I only gave myself five.

Into the office, into the file cabinet. No sweat, the combinations were all listed in numerical order. I'd given myself five minutes and I was out of there in one-and-a-half. Emmett Sundback's locker combination was 16-33-20. I wrote it on the palm of my hand, quickly, with a ballpoint pen, but it wasn't necessary. It had been burned into my brain.

# 32

The radio was the next step. It had to be the best money could buy. Well . . . At least no more than one hundred and ten dollars which was what I had made over the summer. I was ready to spend all of it. It would be worth it.

I found a beauty. AM-FM stereo, two speakers, tape deck, tone control, sleep switch, jack for head-phones, places to hook up more speakers. It also let you record live or off the radio itself. It was really neat—just like one I'd always wanted, though I hadn't planned on getting it this soon.

And then . . .

# 33

Here I was. Walking to the bus stop with the radio, all set to go with the plan. Right in time for Christmas, too, with all my good omens working for me.

Just before I got to the bus stop, I took the radio out from the protection of my jacket and turned it on. I had even tuned it to the station I wanted the night before. Something that would really get attention—a good hard-rock station.

I held it high, even though it was pretty large for a portable, and kind of danced my way over to the wall, closing my eyes and snapping my fingers.

"Hey, nice radio, Bob," one of the seniors called out to me.

"What'ja get, an early Christmas present?" someone else asked, coming over.

Pretty soon, most of the kids at the bus stop were gathered around me admiring the radio. That was the idea, that's why I got one that was so admirable.

Sundback didn't come over, but I didn't expect him to. Neimeier said, "Nice sound!" and Brian Denny said, "That's really a beauty." Kuhn and Gustafson and Levoy kind of smiled. It wasn't because of me. It was the radio. You couldn't ignore it, it was a class act.

When the bus arrived, all the kids begged me to keep it on so I did and that one morning there was no noise on the bus. Everyone just listened. And everyone knew it was mine.

Getting off the bus at school, something happened which I couldn't have planned if I'd tried, but it was just perfect. Sundback bumped into me, almost knocking the radio out of my hand, but not quite. As I drew in my breath and clutched it, he snorted, "You sure like to show off how much money you got, don'tcha, Cherno?"

I smiled. Everyone heard that, too.

My heart was smashing inside my chest. It was during lunch: the moment I'd waited so long for. This was a piece of cake, this was a snap. Just as long as no one saw me. Or even if they did, seeing me opening up a locker was such a normal thing it wouldn't register. Whoever saw me wouldn't know it wasn't my locker and of course, they wouldn't see the radio, which was wrapped in that brown paper I'd taken from Emmett's yard.

Still, it would be better if no one saw me.

Luck was with me all the way! Not a soul in the hall! Everyone was either in class or the cafeteria. I got Sundback's locker open and slipped my package in, placing it carefully on the floor and then piling his books and papers on top of it. I closed the door . . . clicked the combination lock back into place . . . stepped away quickly . . . dared to look around. No one. No one at all.

Next I slipped into the cafeteria, making sure to sit fairly near the door. That way no one would see me and notice if I was or wasn't carrying a radio and also, near the door is where things can easily be ripped off because the thief just splits quick!

Luck was still with me. The lunch period was in full swing. Emmett and Eugene and a few of his other "pals" were horsing around at a table in the middle of the room. Soon Emmett would have to leave by himself. I was watching so intently out of the corner of my eye I jumped when I heard my name called.

"Hey, Bobby, what are you dreaming about? Mind if we sit down?"

I whirled around. They must have thought I was on something—Matty and her girlfriend Liza.

"Uh, what?" I managed.

Matty grinned. "Did I scare you? Sorry. I just asked if Liza and I could sit here."

I wanted her to sit with me so badly I couldn't stand it, but not then. Why did she have to pick *then!*

"Gee, Matty, I'd like—I mean—any other time . . . I'm just—" I was stammering. I couldn't help it. "I have to save . . . the seats . . . just today, Matty . . ."

"Oh. Well, excuse us," she said.

"I'm sorry, really," I called after her weakly. I was, too. So, so sorry.

But if Matty sat down and we started talking she might see that there was no radio on the floor at my feet. Or stashed on the rungs of my chair. Or anywhere else I'd decided to say it was.

I'd make it up to Matty, I would. But now it was time for the plan and only the plan.

I saw Emmett get up from his seat. This was it.

He returned his tray, then began to head in my direction, toward the door. I got up then with my own tray and made as if to return it, dropping a napkin on the floor on my way. It had to be a napkin, not a cup or something that would make an attention-getting sound. Just a piece of paper that I could bend down to get: something to take me out of Sundback's sightline for a minute until he was gone.

I looked up. It was over. Sundback had left. I returned the tray and walked back to my table. I looked down at the floor and all around, counting to ten slowly. Then I drew in my breath in a loud gasp.

"Hey!" I yelled to no one in particular. "Hey! It's gone!"

"What is?" a kid at the other end of my table asked.

"My—my radio! It was right here on the floor when I went to put back my tray! Right here!" I pointed down.

Some of the kids began to stare at me. That's

when I looked over at the table where Emmett had sat. Eugene and the others were still there.

"Sundback's gone, isn't he?" I said. I didn't wait for anyone to answer, but took off immediately for the junior high.

I had done everything right. The next thing was to confront Sundback himself. If he were cutting class, it would only help my story. If he were there, I'd have to face him and accuse him and that would be hard, but I was ready. It was worth it, all of it. I'd have done anything just to be able to watch his face when it all came down on him.

He was just going into the English classroom when I got there. I knew I couldn't stall. I was supposed to be upset out of my mind and I had to act that way. I ran right up to him and grabbed his arm.

"Okay, Sundback," I said, menacingly. "Let's have it, I know it was you!"

He jerked his arm away. "Get out of here, Cherno," he muttered.

"Don't pull that on me," I said. "You went too far this time."

"You're crazy," he said and started to walk into the room. I stayed right with him. A few kids were stopping to listen.

"You ripped off my radio in the cafeteria," I said.

"Hey, you're *really* crazy, get away from me," he said.

It was good, it would work. He absolutely

didn't have an alibi because he left the cafeteria alone. I had him. I knew it.

"This isn't just name-calling or note-writing, Sundback," I said. "I spent a lot of time earning that radio. You got away with all the other stuff, but you're not getting away with this!"

"I don't know what you're talking about," he said, still trying to sound cool, but I could tell he wasn't.

Knowing he couldn't do it, I stood there and dared him. "You give it back to me, I won't say anything. You don't and I'm going right to Wardwell."

"You're crazy!" he said again, and to the kids who were watching, "Hey, he's crazy!"

"Yeah? Everybody on the lake knows all the crap you pulled on me," I said. "But this is one time you lose. Do I get it back or do I tell?"

"I don't have your goddam radio," he growled and almost ran into the classroom.

I looked around at the junior high kids who were standing there. One of the faces was Peggy Kuhn's, Tim's sister. As soon as I saw her expression I knew that Emmett Sundback and the Chernos had made for an interesting Kuhn-family discussion. I could just tell. I connected Peggy's expression with Tim's staying away from the Sundback gang.

"I know he was the one who took it," I said to Peggy. "I just know it." And then I turned and ran out of the building.

*     *     *

"I need to see Mrs. Wardwell . . ."

"Do you have an appointment?"

"No, but . . . I have to see her right away. It's an emergency, honest, Mrs. Kinney . . ."

"What's your name, please?"

"Robert Cherno."

"Just a moment . . ."

She went into the principal's office and came out a couple of seconds later.

"All right, Robert," she said and nodded toward the principal's door.

"Mrs. Wardwell . . ." I began, hesitantly, and then I twisted my lips and shuffled my feet. "This is really hard for me, Mrs. Wardwell . . ."

"What is it, Bobby? If I can help, I'd be glad to. Just sit down and relax a little."

I sat down. Mrs. Wardwell knew my father pretty well. They had once taught in the same school. She would probably listen to me more than just any old kid who was about to accuse someone of theft.

When I didn't speak, she leaned forward over her desk.

I opened and shut my mouth a few times.

"Don't be afraid, Bobby, you can tell me. What is it?"

"I—oh, gee—"

She smiled pleasantly and folded her hands. *Now*, I thought.

"I bought a radio. With the money I spent all summer earning . . ." I began.

"Uh-huh?"

"I brought it to school this morning. I was

really proud of it, Mrs. Wardwell, probably should
have left it home . . ."

"What happened to it?"

"It was stolen," I said.

"Are you sure?"

"Yeah, I'm sure. I know who did it, too, but I
can't prove it."

"Why don't you tell me about it," she said,
like one of those movie psychiatrists.

"I had it near my chair in the cafeteria. I went
to dump my tray and when I got back to my seat
the radio was gone. And so was this kid."

Mrs. Wardwell sighed. This wasn't the problem she had in mind when she saw me come in.

"But you didn't see the person actually take
your radio?"

"I didn't actually see it. But I know who it
was. I know for sure, Mrs. Wardwell."

She unfolded her hands and folded them again.
"Whom do you suspect, Bobby?" she asked.

"Emmett Sundback."

"Oh," she said, and sighed again. I could tell
she knew it was possible. His junior high record
was probably well known.

"He's not walking around with it, that's for
sure," I said. "I just ran down to the junior high
and confronted him, but he denied it."

"Bobby, I just don't know what we can do
about it."

"There is something you can do, Mrs. Wardwell, you can call him in and make him tell."

"Oh, Bobby, now how can I do that?"

I bit my lip. It would be better if the locker-search idea came from someone other than me, but if I had to, I could always suggest it.

"Couldn't you just call him in here? You could talk to him with me here. Maybe he'd admit it then. I'll bet anything he'd admit it if I accused him in front of you!"

"Well . . . I can call him down," she said. "If there's a dispute between two students it's better it be here. All right, I'll have him paged."

Good, I thought. Oh, good . . .

He came in looking scared. Adults really did get to him, he just couldn't hide it.

"Emmett, do you know why I've called you down here?"

"He says I took his radio," he muttered without looking at me. "I never touched his lousy radio."

"I know it was you," I said quietly. "You took it when I went to put my tray back. When I came back to my place it was gone and so were you. All the other kids were there."

"I left early to go to class!" he cried. "I always do!"

"You left early to stash my radio," I said as quietly as before.

"You really are crazy, Cherno!" It was his only comeback. But this time, he did lift his head to look at me.

"Where would I stash it?" He held out his hands. "Where would I put it? In my shirt?"

"Maybe the same place where you keep your black paint," I whispered.

"You goddam kike-liar!" he screamed. Mrs. Wardwell gasped.

I sucked in air, too. I hadn't expected that, but I might have. I goaded him too much.

"I think we'll have a look in your locker, Emmett," Mrs. Wardwell said, and I closed my eyes. He'd done it to himself, cooked his own goose. Mrs. Wardwell didn't have to humor the possibly innocent any more, all bets were off.

"I'msorryIsaidthat," Emmett said, all in one breath. "He got me mad. I didn't take his damn— his radio and I just got mad." He was looking at the floor.

"I don't care how mad you got, young man," Mrs. Wardwell said. "There are other ways of expressing your anger. Do you object to having your locker examined?"

"No! No, I don't object! Go search it, go on, then you'll be sorry!"

I had buried it well in my few allotted seconds. And the paper did cover it, but it looked like it was one hasty wrap-job. I took a mental photograph of the three of us when Mrs. Wardwell uncovered the radio. Her face, my face—and Emmett Sundback's.

# 34

No one believed him. Not even any of the kids who were supposed to be his friends. They didn't hate him for "stealing," they just didn't believe he hadn't done it.

The thing is, because of everything that Emmett had done to me, stealing my radio was just natural in the succession of things as far as people were concerned. Any kind of slips I might have made, anything that didn't quite jell—all of those things were overlooked because what Emmett supposedly did was what was expected of Emmett. Eugene called him stupid for getting caught.

Sundback never said a word to me, not a whisper, not a threat. He hardly even said a word in defense of himself!

And, of course, he was suspended from school.

"I'd love to press criminal charges," my father said. "That would give me the greatest pleasure!"

"No," I said. "I think he's been punished enough. The whole school knows he's a thief.

And I got the radio back. He got his, you can let it go, Dad."

My mother said, "I told you not to take the radio to school, Bobby . . ."

I just kept petting Nasty.

# 35

It was over. I pulled it off. I had started planning it in September and I made it work in December. I kept telling myself how smart I was, how right I was. I did it! And with Sundback hardly saying anything at all, it was as if he were playing right along with it! Now here was Christmas vacation and Sundback wouldn't be in school when it started again! The thing is, I didn't feel as sensational as I thought I would, or as terrific as I felt while I was planning the whole thing and even while I was carrying it out.

And there was no one I could tell about it.

We went to Florida again. I tried to put the whole thing out of my mind, but I couldn't. It didn't seem like a whole year had passed since we had been there or seen Grandma, but it had. Some year.

It wasn't the same down there for me. I swam a little . . . but by myself. Dad would ask me to go sailing with him or fish or anything and somehow I just didn't . . . couldn't . . . go with him.

"Hey, Bob, what's wrong?" he'd ask. "What's on your mind?"

I couldn't tell him and I couldn't be with him. My mother was worried, too. She talked to me a lot. A *lot*. It was as if she were afraid of the silence there'd be if she didn't do the talking. She'd ask me questions and then when I didn't answer right away she'd answer for me, filling in the blank, like in a quiz.

"Bobby, don't you feel well?" she'd ask, touching my head.

"Fine," I'd tell her. I couldn't look at her, either.

"Is it Emmett Sundback again?"

And when I didn't answer, she'd say, "Well, it couldn't be. Not down here."

I tried, really I did. But I just wanted to be by myself. Grandma was the only one who seemed satisfied with a hug and kiss every now and then and didn't nag at me to join in something.

It was pretty ironic, that vacation. Last year when I was miserable, I had a wonderful time and ate like a horse. Now this year when I'm happy, all I seemed to do was walk on the beach and pick up shells.

I didn't get it.

Things were fine back at school. During the week, Matty came right up to me in study hall. I hadn't spoken to her since the day in the cafeteria, the day of the radio. But she's so nice—she never mentioned it at all.

"Bobby, I heard what Emmett Sundback did

to you," she said. "It made me feel just awful. I
remember what happened when we went out
last year, too. He's a pig. I can't stand him.
Nobody can. He's suspended this week, isn't
he?"

"Yeah," I mumbled. It was like with my parents in Florida. I was having trouble looking at
Matty, too.

"I guess it was Emmett who painted your car
like that, too, wasn't it?" she asked.

I shrugged.

"Yeah, you're too nice to say anything bad,
but I know."

I smiled. Or tried to.

"You know," she said, "if we ever went out
again, we could get one of our fathers to drive
us out of the area somewhere, so we wouldn't
have to run into people like Emmett later . . .
You know?"

"Are you asking me out?" I said with a smile.

"Well . . ." She shrugged. "I just thought
maybe our going out was an annual event. I
mean, Christmas vacation comes, you go to
Florida, get a nice tan, you come back, we go
out . . . . It's just that time of year, right?"

I nodded. "Right," I said. "Right . . ."

Now I was supposed to feel excited and happy
and suggest a day and time and something to do.
I *was* happy, I liked Matty, she was one of the
nicest people I'd ever met, and one of the
prettiest. Only I wasn't saying anything.

"So?" she said.

"I—I'll call you," I managed.

"Mmmm," she said. "Sure. I'll bet. What's the matter, did your father find out I'm not Jewish?"

"Oh, Matty."

It was no use.

I couldn't feel happy, I couldn't feel sad. I simply couldn't feel anything.

The next Monday I braced myself for Sundback's return to the bus stop—only he wasn't there. I had mixed feelings about it. I was glad not to see him, of course, but I knew his suspension was up and I'd have to face him sometime . . . I guess I just wanted to get it over with.

It was weighing on me so much I even thought I saw him, Sundback, in the cafeteria during lunch, but I knew it couldn't be. I was getting spooked, that's how much things were getting to me.

Coming home that afternoon, I got off the school bus quickly, as usual, and headed down toward the lake, when I heard my name being called. I turned around to see Brian running toward me. I thought, what does *he* want?

"Wait up!" he called, and caught up to me, panting. "I looked for you on the bus. Where were you?"

"I was there," I mumbled.

We started to walk. "You hear what happened to Sundback?" Brian asked.

I looked at him sharply. "No . . ."

"His father beat him up so bad he was in the hospital practically the whole Christmas vacation.

So guess what, his mother took him back to live with her."

I thought numbly, so I *did* see him in the cafeteria. He's back, he just won't be on the bus any more. Fine. I still couldn't feel anything.

"Yeah, well, I thought you'd like to hear that news," Brian said with a grin. I looked away from my friend Brian—now Sundback's good friend, too.

"Anyway," he went on, "you know why he got it? His father was pissed at him for getting in trouble again."

I looked up. "That's why he beat him up? Because he was suspended from school? For taking my radio?"

"That's right!" The idiot was still grinning.

I walked quickly away from him.

"Hey, what's wrong with *you?*" he called after me. "I wanted to be the one to bring you the news!"

# 36

I didn't feel good and couldn't feel good. Not only about Sundback getting his, but about *anything*. I kept going over it and over it in my head. I had really taken it all year from Sundback, and not just me, Bob Cherno, but Jews in general with me as their representative. Sundback deserved to be punished for that; it's like games: there are rules for playing games and there are rules for living life, and one of the rules is you don't hate people for their race or color or religion or anything like that. And if you do hate somebody because of their race or color or religion, then you're not allowed to do anything to them, like persecute them in any way. It's in the Constitution, it's why the Pilgrims came here, it's a rule, it's a law.

Sundback broke the rule. No question about it. And because I was the one he picked to break it with, then it was up to me to handle it, without dragging other people into it. And I did, I handled it by using my brains and figuring out a way to get him back. The plan worked, it all

155

worked, just the way I had it mapped out. It cost
me weeks and weeks of hard thought, not to mention one hundred and ten dollars for the radio,
and it all worked!

Then why was I walking around like a zombie?

My mother must have felt my head eighty
times, but I told her it was upcoming exams that
were making me so preoccupied.

I decided I had to get rid of the radio. I could
barely look at it and I certainly couldn't *play* it.
It was making me sick. I decided to return it to
the store, get rid of it, get the whole thing out of
my sight and my mind.

But I couldn't even do that!

"Gee, I'm sorry, son," the clerk said. "It's
past time for Christmas returns."

"But it's in great shape, honest!" I said, almost in tears.

"Then why do you want to return it?" the
clerk said and smiled.

Alone in my room that night, I started to
pace. A thought struck me so hard that I had to
sit down quick. *Was I feeling sorry for Emmett
Sundback?* I buried my face in my hands. Think,
Bobby, think—is that what you're feeling? Are
you pitying him?

I thought. I pictured last year. I pictured the
summer. And I knew that wasn't it, I wasn't
feeling sorry for him. I was feeling sorry that
what I did to pay him back didn't really pay him
back!

He was suspended from school, sure, but not

for something he did, like calling me "kike." It was for stealing something he never stole. He got beaten for that, too, for something he wasn't even responsible for.

I would have felt okay if his punishment, or whatever you want to call it, fit what he did and made him sorry. That would have been right.

But what I did wasn't right, I knew it. It had nothing to do with what Emmett had done to me. Besides even that—I guess I had to admit to myself that the main thing I was feeling was guilt. I wasn't sorry for Sundback, I don't think I could ever be sorry for him no matter what, but I was sorry for myself—that what I had done was so sneaky and didn't really solve anything, besides.

Once I finally said it—not out loud, just to myself—I felt better about one thing: understanding it. I hadn't been able to look my parents in the eye, I hadn't been able to look at the stupid radio, I hadn't been able to even smile at Matty Greeley. Now I understood why a little better but I didn't know what to do about it.

When you feel guilty I guess what you want to do is talk to someone. Only there wasn't a soul in the entire world I could tell. I thought if I were Catholic then I could at least go to confession, but then again, if I were Catholic, then I wouldn't have had the problem in the first place. Sundback didn't hate Catholics—at least as far as I knew.

I tried to picture the looks on my mother's and father's faces when I told them it was all a lie, all a setup, Emmett never stole the radio, I planted it on him. What would they think? What would anybody's parents think if their son told them a thing like that?

I shivered. I couldn't do it, I couldn't, I couldn't, I couldn't.

Who, then?

There was only one other living human being who knew that Bob Cherno's radio was not stolen by Emmett Sundback and that was Emmett Sundback.

Emmett.

Maybe talking to Emmett was the answer!

# 37

The more I thought it through, the more I felt it was right, I would confess what I'd done, even though I knew he knew, and then we'd finally be able to talk. I'd say, "Look Emmett, the slate's clean now. You were rotten to me all year and you called me a lot of bad names . . ." and then I'd go on to point out to him that as a person and as a Jew, I just couldn't go on taking his crap, and so I had to do something. I wouldn't point out how much planning it took, but he would know and maybe even respect me a little for it, like enemies sometimes respect the strategies of each other.

Maybe it would make him look at Jews differently. Maybe he would think of us as resourceful and also, if I came to him and confessed, as open and forgiving . . . I stopped right there. Maybe what he'd want is for me to go to Mrs. Wardwell and confess. He hadn't really tried to defend himself at all, so maybe he'd want me to do it. Maybe he hadn't said anything because he knew he wouldn't be believed. He *wasn't* believed, even by his so-called friends.

What would I do if he told me to go to Mrs. Wardwell? I began to bite my nail. He would want that, I thought, and I suppose I couldn't blame him. But anyway, at least his opinion of me and of Jews would be different.

No matter what happened, I decided the thing to do was to go right to Emmett himself. Everything would be all right after that.

I slept well for the first time in weeks. I'd get to him the very next day.

# 38

For the first time since the radio thing I sought out Emmett Sundback.

I can only describe my feelings as excited, nervous and almost relieved, all mixed together. I had been jumpy all morning—I couldn't wait to talk to him.

It wasn't until after school that I caught up with him. He was staying for wrestling, and even though it meant I'd miss my bus, I figured I could probably catch an activity bus after four o'clock.

He was just going into the gym when I called his name.

"Whadda *you* want," he growled when he saw who it was.

"I just want to talk to you a minute," I said in a serious tone. "Just talk. That's it."

He sauntered over, twisting his mouth and looking around as he walked.

"What," he said.

"I know you're sore about what happened."

"What—?"

"Wait a minute, that's what I want to talk about . . ." I looked at him carefully, but I didn't see any signs of a beating or that he'd even been hurt at all. Maybe it was just in parts that didn't show . . . Well—it had been three weeks ago . . .

"Look, Emmett . . . It's about the radio," I said.

He didn't say anything . . . just stood there, kind of sneering at me.

I went on quickly. "I was the one who put it there . . . in your locker. Did you—I mean . . . You knew that, didn't you?"

The sneer on his face didn't change, but it seemed frozen to me. I wasn't very sure of what he was thinking so I kept on talking.

"Anyway, you never really defended yourself. You said you didn't do it, but you never pushed it . . . You never asked for a hearing or anything, you never defended yourself."

He tossed his head and snorted. "Why should I?" he jeered. "It was like a favor. Got me out of school for an extra week. I had a long vacation while you suckers sat in the sweathole!"

I swallowed. It wasn't what I'd expected him to say. I didn't know what to do next, but I felt I should keep talking. I wanted things to fall into place, to get squared, to make it all stop.

"Listen," I said. "I'm sorry you got a beating for what I—" That was as far as I got. His face turned purple.

"Who told you I got hit!" he cried. "You dirty, sneaky, lyin—" He pulled me close by my shirt collar. His lips were pulled back and I could see his teeth clamped together. Then he whispered right into my face.

"I can't afford to be in any more trouble because of you, you slimy little Hebe, or I'd plaster you against this wall right now!" He did push me up against the wall but then he let me go.

My head was reeling but I kept talking.

"Hey, look, those names you called me were what made me do it! You can't go around hating and picking on someone because they're Jewish or—"

"Who says I can't!" He made a spitting noise at the floor. "You stupid Jew-sap, who says I can't!"

The wrestling coach was coming down the hall. Sundback's eyes glinted with fear. He whirled quickly and disappeared into the gym.

I stood there against the wall, shaking.

It wasn't right, none of it was right, I never said everything I had planned to say, or at least it hadn't come out right, and he never said *anything* that he was supposed to say . . .

It hadn't worked and I was right back where I was before, only worse.

"Hi, honey, how was the history exam?" Mom asked me when I got home from school.

The history exam. I'd been glad to have it. The studying and the exams were the only things that got my mind off being miserable.

"It was okay," I said. "It was fine."

"Oh, good, keep it up, honey. By the way, I found your brand new radio in the laundry room this afternoon when I got home from school."

"Oh. Yeah."

"What was it doing there?"

"I tried to return it but the store wouldn't take it back. They said I had it too long."

"Why did you want to return it? You worked so hard for it, I thought you loved it!"

"I did, I—aw—"

"Come in here." She took my by the arm and led me into the living room where she sat down on the couch and patted the cushion next to her. I sat, too.

"Let's have it right now. I can't take any more of this secrecy that eats you up alive. Independence is just fine, but you're carrying it too far. I'm asking—no, I'm demanding—that you tell me what's going on. Right now. Whatever it is, I don't care what it is, you know I'm going to be behind you one hundred percent. So let's have it."

I couldn't look at her. How could she be behind me one hundred percent when—if—I told her everything. I'd lose her, too, I'd lose everybody.

"Bobby?"

But maybe that's what I deserved. Maybe I just deserved to be found out and just lose everything and everybody.

Just then my father walked through the front door and I knew that was an omen. I'd tell. I'd tell both of them together and to hell with it.

\*   \*   \*

I talked until almost six. I told them everything. About what really happened to Nasty Cat and about Brian Denny, Tim Kuhn and Cliff Neimeier—all their friends and neighbors—but I had to. This time I couldn't hold back, because every bit of it was part of what led me into Sundback's locker that day so it had to come out if I expected my parents to see any sense in it at all. And after I told them the stuff that led up to it, I painted the rest of the picture: how I'd planned, schemed, worked and carried it out, right up to my great little talk with Sundback near the gym.

When I was finished they just sat there, sometimes looking at each other, sometimes staring into space, but not looking at me. I looked at each of them, though. For the first time in weeks, I could look right at them.

Finally, my father spoke.

"Why are you telling us now?" he asked very quietly.

"Because I couldn't stand how I was feeling and I didn't know what to do."

My father stood up. He shook his head and kind of smiled in a funny way. "Brian Denny?" he said, still shaking his head.

I nodded.

"And Tim Kuhn!" my mother said. "Imagine!"

"Kuhn was different after the newspaper story," I said. "And I saw Peggy in school, too, and she gave me a kind of knowing look . . .

Kuhn's stopped hanging around the group this year, I hardly see him except at the bus."

"Sure, but before, the Kuhn boy was right in with them," my father said.

"Yeah . . ."

My mother looked at him. "None of them understood. None of them realized. The Kuhn boy, Brian—all of them. They didn't know. They just followed the bully. Mindlessly. Look! There's a leader, let's go follow him . . ."

They were quiet for a while. I kept watching them. It felt so good not to always have to look away and not meet their eyes.

"You had a rough time, Bob," my father said finally.

I didn't answer.

"Did you expect that after you told us this story . . . that we would punish you for what you'd done?"

"I don't know," I answered. "I don't know what I expected. I was just feeling so awful for so long I had to tell you, that's all." I felt tears coming. I hadn't really cried all the time Sundback was on me, and now all I wanted to do was cry.

"I just don't know," I repeated as the tears washed down my face. "I wanted to punish Sundback for what he did, only it was a wrong punishment, I should have done something else, only I don't know what—" I was really blubbering now "—and I don't know how to make up for it, especially since I know he deserved *something—*"

"Oh, Bobby—" My mother put her arm around

me. I leaned against her, just like I did when I was a kid.

"Bobby, don't you know you can't punish hatred? You can't take revenge against prejudice, it doesn't make an anti-Semite stop hating Jews."

"Well, what does?"

She shook her head. "There isn't any response, Bobby. There's always going to be hatred. What I tried to do with the newspaper was to make people aware that it was happening here. Those kids that went blindly along with Emmett Sundback—and those kids' families—they needed to know that what they were doing hurts! When people saw that picture of our car in the Middleboro News it reminded them of how painful blind hatred is. That's what I wanted to show."

"But you can't make someone not hate!" I cried.

"No. You can't. But people will get away with acting out their hate unless the pain of it is placed right before everyone's eyes."

My father handed me his handkerchief and I wiped my face.

"But what about me," I mumbled. "What do I do now?"

"I think you know, Bob," my father said.

"Tell Mrs. Wardwell?" I asked, looking up at him.

"I'll go with you," he said.

# 39

So I went through it again. My father didn't interrupt me once. I only found it hard the first few minutes; after that, it came easily, like reciting the lyrics to a song I know well.

I finished talking and Mrs. Wardwell did just what my parents had done—looked away, down at her desk.

Then she said, "Bobby, I think I'd like to have a few words with your father alone. Would you mind waiting in the outer office?"

But my father said, "Sylvia, if it's all right with you, I think it would be better if Bob were here through the whole thing. You can say anything to me, but I'd like him to hear it, too."

"Very well, Jerry, but this is difficult—"

"I know. I know it's difficult," my father said.

"Bobby, what you did was very wrong. And you used me, too."

"I know, Mrs. Wardwell. I didn't want to do that. I'm sorry."

She pursed and unpursed her lips. "The damn dilemma is—" she said with a quick shake of her head, "if this were a cut-and-dried case—a boy frames another boy—I could deal with it in a cut-and-dried way . . ."

"Don't let our friendship interfere, Sylvia," my father said but she put her hand up.

"It isn't our friendship, Jerry, although that would make me feel badly enough about it. It's what the Sundback boy did to Bobby that I'm thinking of. He certainly deserved to be punished—"

I looked at my father.

"My mother says you can't change prejudice by punishing it," I said.

"Ah, yes, well . . ." She shook her head again. "Believe me, Bobby, I'm not condoning what you did."

"I'm not either," I said. "I've been feeling—" I took a deep breath. "That's why I'm telling you about it. I just want to get this feeling out of me."

"I don't like what you did but I don't like what you went through, either," she said, standing up. "And if it happened to you it could happen to any other student right here at Middleboro. If you had just come to me when it first began . . ."

"You weren't my principal last year," I said lamely.

"You know what I mean, Bobby. And you could have come *this* year . . ."

"I couldn't!" I cried. "Don't you see?"

"I see. I know how kids are, you never 'rat' on anyone no matter what they do."

"Oh, yeah," I said, "that's part of it. The whole

school thinks you're a fink and that's your reputation forever. Yeah, that was part of it, but it was more. I just felt that it was my problem, I didn't want others fighting my battles for me. And besides, it wouldn't have changed Emmett anyway, we know that now."

She nodded, she kept nodding. Then she sat back down at her desk.

"Bobby, you've put me in the position of acting as judge here," she said. "I'm afraid I'm going to have to call the Sundback boy down."

"I don't mind," I said. I think I was still hoping that talking it out would make it better with Emmett.

While we were waiting, we discussed whether or not my father should stay in the room. I remembered that night at Emmett's house and I thought maybe it would look like we were ganging up on him or something. But they said that my father was in on it, that it was his problem, too, so he stayed. I squirmed around till the door opened and Emmett came in.

His face was white anyway, but he took one look at me and my father and I thought he was really going to faint. He didn't say a word.

"Sit down, Emmett," Mrs. Wardwell said, and he did. Immediately. As if she'd hit him if he didn't.

"Emmett, I know now that you were innocent, that you did not steal Bobby Cherno's radio," she began. "I know that Bobby framed you."

Emmett glanced at me through the corner of

his eye quickly. Then he looked back at the principal.

"I also know what led Bobby to do what he did."

Emmett swallowed. I saw his Adam's apple move.

"Do you know what 'bigotry' means, Emmett, and what it can lead to?"

Emmett didn't answer. He just kept staring at her.

"Bobby's father is here because you've made him a victim of your prejudice, too. When you picked on Bobby, you picked on all Jews, Emmett. You've taken on a lot of so-called enemies for yourself, haven't you?"

Emmett opened his mouth and then closed it.

"You're here, Emmett, because I'd like to hear what you have to say. You certainly should have your say. You became a victim yourself, didn't you?"

Emmett seemed to shrink into his chair. He didn't answer.

"Don't you want to say anything?" Mrs. Wardwell said. "Bobby has told us about the cheating, the swastika, the cat, the chants and the jeers, the other boys . . . Is any of it made up, Emmett?"

Nothing from Emmett. I just kept thinking that any other kid would either be denying or apologizing, breaking down, *something!* Not Sundback, he just sat there.

"I'm trying to be fair, Emmett. I heard you myself, that day in my office. I heard the name you called him. Don't you want to talk about it? Do you want to say something about Bobby? About the way you feel about Jews?"

She waited. Then she sighed.

"All right, Emmett. I wanted to give you a chance. You may go back to your classroom now."

Emmett leaped to his feet as though someone had lit a match under him.

He pulled open the door and started to leave. But something held him in the doorway.

"Yes, Emmett?" Mrs. Wardwell said hopefully.

He took a breath. "I didn't do anything today . . ." he said gruffly. "Are you going to tell my father I got called down here?"

Mrs. Wardwell closed her eyes. "No, Emmett," she said.

Then he was gone.

"Nothing registered," my father said. "Nothing. Only what his father would do to him."

Mrs. Wardwell didn't say anything. I didn't know what she knew or didn't know about Emmett's father, but whatever it was she didn't discuss it with us. She didn't mention Emmett again, she talked only to me.

"It's obvious to me, Bobby," she said, "that you are aware that yours was a terrible act of revenge and very, very wrong. I know that telling your parents, coming here and telling me, was difficult for you but the guilt you must be feeling made you do it. So it's my belief that you've been punished enough by your own sense of decency—you're a good boy. But I'm not finished with this whole situation. I need some time to think it through, find some way for us all to come to terms with it."

"But how?" I said. I felt let down again. Each time I tried to do something to make it all better it just seemed to fall through! Trying to return the radio, talking to Emmett, telling my parents, the principal—nothing was resolving anything!

"What are you going to do, Mrs. Wardwell?" I asked. I hoped I wasn't whining.

"Bobby, I don't know yet. I told you, I need time."

I looked at my father. "Is there anything that *can* be done, Dad?" I asked.

He didn't answer, either.

# 40

After a few days, Mrs. Wardwell called me to the office. My heart was pounding and I thought about the way Emmett probably felt when he was called. I had never been afraid before when the principal wanted to see me and now I was.

"Bobby, I want you to know that first thing tomorrow morning, we're going to have a special assembly in the auditorium," she said to me. "I'm telling you about it in advance, though I'm sure you'll know when you see it, that this is one thing I've decided to do about everything you've told me. I'm sure you'll find it quite a revelation."

A revelation! I nearly stopped breathing.

"An assembly?" I asked. It came out a croak. "An assembly in front of the whole school? The whole school, Mrs. Wardwell?"

"Oh, Bobby, don't worry. It isn't going to be personal. That wouldn't solve anything."

"But what do you mean, how can it not be personal? Emmett—the things he did—they were to *me*. The radio, *I* planted it. You can't get more personal than that! Aw, Mrs. Wardwell, if

I was hated before, just think what everyone will do now!"

But all she said was not to worry, not to worry.

The next day I told my parents I was sick. It was true. And I told them I wasn't going to school.

"Yes you are, Bobby," my mother said. "You are going to school. And so are we. There's going to be a special assembly—"

"You know about it?"

"Yes, honey, and your dad's going to be speaking."

"*At my school?*"

"Come on, Bob," he said. "We'll drive you."

I huddled miserably in the back seat. I kept thinking stupid things, like "the next time I see this street it'll be all over," and usually thoughts like that helped, but since I didn't know what it was that would be all over, nothing worked. Every time I asked my parents what the assembly was for all they said was not to worry. Like Mrs. Wardwell. It would be all right, they said. It wasn't about the radio. Mrs. Wardwell had an idea. A lesson for everybody. I slumped even more in my seat.

When we got to school I practically leaped out of the car and ran for my homeroom . . . I didn't want to go into assembly with my parents, whatever happened.

\* \* \*

I was sitting with my class, not far from the aisle. My hands felt cold and I tucked them under my armpits as I stared at the stage. The large screen was pulled down and I wondered why.

Shortly before the noise calmed down, Brian poked me in the back.

"Hey, Cherno, your parents are here."

I nodded, but I guess he didn't see.

"Hey," he repeated, "I said your parents are here. They just walked in. They're in the back."

"Yeah, I know, Denny."

Mrs. Wardwell suddenly appeared on the stage, under the screen. She tapped and blew into the microphone on the podium. It whistled loudly and made the kids cover their ears.

"Sorry," she said. "I hope this is better. Can everyone hear me?"

"Yes Mis-sus Wardwell," came the chorus.

"Good. Now, what you're all about to see is going to shock you. No matter what you've heard or read before, I promise you that you will be shocked. I'm saying this to prepare you, I don't doubt that it will happen."

The auditorium was completely hushed now.

"I want it to happen," she went on. "I want you all—" she emphasized the word "all" and peered around the auditorium—"to be so upset by what will be shown on this screen that you will never forget it throughout your lives. I want this to be one of the most important school lessons any of you will ever have."

She paused. No one spoke during the pause.

A couple of kids looked at each other quizzically but only for a second.

"These are films," Mrs. Wardwell went on, "that record history. But it won't be history if we allow ourselves to forget about it. If we don't remember—all the time—then that history will soon become a present agony.

"The films were taken at the close of the Second World War, at several concentration camps, shortly after the Allies liberated them. Two of their names are Auschwitz and Dachau. I want all of you to repeat those names."

"Ausch-witz and Da-chau" the kids chanted.

"They will be more than just words to you in a few minutes," she continued. "The films' narrations will tell you the rest."

Sundback was sitting two rows behind me. I had looked for him more out of habit than anything else.

As Mrs. Wardwell finished and the lights dimmed, I took one last look at him.

The film began. First we saw heaps—great piles of things that had belonged to the camp occupants: clothing, jewelry, toys—anything, the narrator said, that gave one a sense of individuality. There were also gold fillings. From teeth.

The camera moved on to more heaps, this time of bodies that had been piled haphazardly, naked people on top of naked people, arms, legs, heads . . . faces. Children.

The narrator said that parents used to instruct the children to hide under the piles of bodies when the guards came to get them . . . the children hid under the dead people so they wouldn't be found . . .

Then we saw the survivors. They stood together in dark rows, their eyes large and gaping. Many of them were naked. We saw their bones, their ribs, their jutting bellies, distended from starvation. Their heads were shaved, their arms and legs—sticks.

A girl cried out.

The narrator said more but I wasn't listening.

Then the screen went dark and the lights came up.

I had seen many movies, many shows, many guest speakers in that auditorium. Whenever the lights came up, there was the usual pandemonium of kids in a group with a minute free. Not now. There was not a sound.

I turned around toward Emmett Sundback. He was sitting, staring straight ahead like every other kid in his row, in all the rows, waiting for the next film. His face wore no expression at all. I glanced back further, but I didn't see my parents. That was all right.

Behind me, Brian was picking his nails. Art Levoy looked over at me and shook his head, as if to say, "Wow." Two girls across the aisle from me were crying. I began to look for Matty, but I couldn't see her.

I got up out of my seat. "May I go get a drink?" I asked my teacher at the end of the aisle.

"Sure, go ahead, Bobby," he said.

I walked to the very back of the auditorium, nodded to my mother who nodded back with a tiny smile and then I scanned the place for swinging shoulder-length hair. I spotted her not far from where I was sitting. Quickly, I got my drink and then came back in, walking slowly down the aisle, my eyes on Matty Greeley. She turned and saw me and we just looked at each other. That was all. She looked solemn, but she wasn't crying. Suddenly I wanted very much to be with her again.

The lights were dimming. I found my seat.

Before us on the screen were more people, if you could still call them that. They were expressionless shells of human beings.

The women had gaping crevices where there should have been breasts. The men had no penises. Some of the children were legless, some armless, some totally limbless. The young girls, the narrator said, had had their ovaries removed. All of their heads were shaved, they were bald. They were staring at the camera, at the person who was filming them, and their eyes all looked like black holes.

" . . . the results," the narrator was saying, "of experiments performed on the Jews in the camps by Nazi doctors."

I had heard about the "experiments." "Experiments" the A.S.P.C.A. wouldn't have permitted on animals. The horrors of the camps . . . Sure, I'd heard about them. But Mrs. Wardwell was right—no matter what you heard, you couldn't imagine what was real.

The camera moved on. The gas chambers that the Jews were told were "showers." The place where the orchestra, comprised of prominent Jewish women musicians, played and had to watch as scores were marched off to die.

When the film showed a small child with burnholes all over its body, Cliff Neimeier got up and left so fast he stepped on my foot hard as he pushed through the row.

"Sorry. Sorry, Cherno," he murmured as I gasped.

What are you sorry for, Cliff, I thought.

Someone else rushed up the aisle, I couldn't see who. Some kids were crying openly, all around me. I could hear the sniffles and sobs but nothing drowned out the sound of the narrator.

When two more students walked up the aisle toward the door, Mrs. Wardwell appeared suddenly on the stage. "Don't leave!" she said sharply, the distorted screen images dancing across her body. "Do not leave now!"

"She's sick, Mrs. Wardwell," a girl's voice called back and the two were allowed out into the hall.

At last the second film ended. There was another one but one of the teachers stood up and suggested that two films had been enough. I craned my neck to get a glimpse of Sundback again but his chair was empty.

Mrs. Wardwell had walked to her microphone again.

"One of the teachers feels that you've all seen enough," she said.

There were nods and mumbles this time, no chant of agreement.

"All right." She paused and looked around. It seemed like she wanted to look into every single face.

Then she continued. "At this time, I'd like to introduce Mr. Jerome Cherno—"

Here it was. My stomach lurched.

"—who would like to address you."

My father strode to the stage. I cringed. It was all too much for me.

"I'd like to talk to you," he began loudly into the microphone, "about the reasons these films were presented to you today. I'd like to talk to you about fear, about prejudice, about—"

I suddenly found myself hyperventilating.

"May I go to the boys' room, please?" I asked as I shoved my way out. I saw the teacher nod but I would have gone anyway. I tried to look as if I weren't racing as I got to the door and leaned heavily against it to get it open.

I relaxed a little only when I was safely inside the bathroom with the door closed.

It was a summary, that was all. A talk for the benefit of the kids about prejudice and bigotry. I even knew it would be good—my father was a good speaker, I'd heard him many times. But he was still my father and this was my school and this was our problem and I had to get out of the auditorium, right then.

I was retroactively sick from the films.

I had read, I had seen pictures, but still—you can't think that what happened could happen.

You can't really believe that human beings could be that incredibly cruel to other human beings. No matter what you hear or read, you can't believe it.

I cleaned up and came out of the boys' room, hoping the speech was over.

Sundback was leaning over the water fountain. He stood up, wiping his mouth on his shirt sleeve, and noticed me at the same time. There was no one in the hall now but us. He smiled.

"Was that for me, Chernowitz?" he asked. "Did you and your daddy set that all up for me?"

"My father—" I started to shout, feeling my face redden and my heart pound. And then I stopped. Emmett was looking at me with his head tilted to one side, mockingly. That's when I knew: there wasn't one word in the English language that would make Emmett Sundback be anything but what he was. There was nothing I could do to him that would make him change except kill him. And even if I could do that it wouldn't kill his ideas. Or the ideas of my parents' superintendent in New York City. Or any other bigot. There wasn't only one Emmett Sundback in the world.

He saw those films. He saw kids right there in the assembly being sick over them, and crying, and everything. But nothing happened to Emmett's insides, nothing. Emmett would go on and on . . .

We were still looking at each other, three feet apart and light-years away. I discovered my fists were clenched tightly and I unclenched them and stood up straighter.

I thought about the assembly, and the kids who cried. There were more of them than the Sundbacks.

"It isn't Chernowitz," I said to Emmett. "My name is Cherno."